MATTHE

LET IT RIDE

To my sister, Erin – the most resilient person I know.

Illustrated by Lizzie Morrison

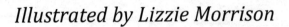

A special thanks to Ken Chamlee, Kristina Holland, Brandon Smith and Jubal Tiner of Brevard College.

Table of Contents

Chapter I

THE OLD SEX GAG - PART ONE

I hate premonitions. When I experience one, I usually find myself at rock bottom within the week. I've had quite a few - including the one I'm having during this very moment. However, this one is a bit different than the others, because when I hit rock bottom a week ago, I was thrown a shovel and told to dig.

For the past week, I've been tied to a chair in the basement of a 99 year-old woman's house. I've been beaten repetitively, drugged, sliced open with both knives and sheets of paper, shot twice, burned, and my mustache was shaved. To top it all off, I've had an old sex gag stuffed in my mouth for the majority of that time. I can already feel the cold sore coming on, and I no longer have a mustache to cover it up.

So, how could things possibly get worse, you ask? My guests, whom I'm expecting to arrive momentarily, will be able to explain that for you.

BAM!

The upstairs door bashed open. There was a stampede of feet rushing through the house, and voices began to yell.

"NYPD! WE HAVE A WARRANT!"

"LIVING ROOM'S CLEAR!"

"BEDROOM'S CLEAR!"

"KITCHEN'S CLEAR!

"BATHROOM'S CLEAR!

"CHECK THE BASEMENT!"

BAM!

The basement door flung open and smashed into the wall.

"I'VE GOT MOVEMENT DOWN HERE," a cop shouted. "LET ME SEE YOUR HANDS! GET ON YOUR KNEES! LET ME SEE YOUR FUCKING HANDS!"

It can always get worse. Remember that. So, how did I get myself into such a predicament? It all started with my desire to 'stick it to the man.' I didn't want to work a 9 to 5. I wanted to do whatever I pleased.

Chapter II

TAPPED OUT

My name is Beau Allen, and I have a gambling problem. What can I say? I'm addicted. I love the buzz that comes with making a bet. I love winning. Most of all, I love letting it ride. When I get that feeling, I trust my gut and throw everything on my next bet.

Recently, I got hot. That's actually an understatement. I was on fire. Every game I picked cashed. If I picked a football team to win by three or more, they'd win by four on a last second touchdown. If I picked a basketball team to win by six or more, they'd drain a three-pointer at the buzzer to win by seven. It was glorious. I was letting it ride left and right. It was the high that I was looking for, and it led to winning $40,000 in a 5-day span.

Unfortunately, all good things must come to an end. I lost the fire. It didn't take long for me to be ice-cold. $100,000 in debt type of ice-cold. It all happened so fast. I have a little over $10,000 in my savings account, and no assets to speak of, other than an old, beat-up, red 98' Honda Accord. Ideally, I'd try to gamble my way out of this hole, but it's Tuesday, and I ante up on Tuesday's.

I moved to Brooklyn a little over a year ago. It's my first time living in the North. I needed a change. I visited my friend, Zuber, in New York, and the bright lights of the city filled my mind with inspiration. I felt as if I had woken from a coma. Moving here was all I could think about, so I made it happen.

The first job I landed was as a telemarketer. When I interviewed for the job, the boss told me that I would be able to work from my apartment. I was sold. The more opportunities one has to wear sweat pants, the better. Unfortunately, it turns out that I'm not what people in sales would refer to as a 'closer.' So, when I got the axe as a telemarketer, I decided that I would roll the dice and go pro in sports gambling. The sweat pants were still in play, and I watched sports for a living. Even better.

Zuber introduced me to my bookie, Johnny Santoro, at Santoro's Sports Bar one Sunday morning an hour before that day's football games kicked off. Prior to being introduced, Zuber told me that Johnny was connected. He's in Arno "The Eagle" Soldetti's mafia family. He ranted about how they call Arno "The Eagle," because he sees absolutely everything that happens beneath him, and he's on top of the world. I always loved mafia movies, so, naturally, I was intrigued. Johnny is also Zuber's bookie, but Zuber only bets 50 dollars per game, to keep it interesting.

While I was telemarketing, I made $100 per game. After I went pro, I moved up to $500 - $5,000 per game, depending on my confidence-level. Overall, excluding this week, I've made money. Well, let me rephrase that. I've been able to pay the rent. The most I've ever won in a week was $30,000, and the most I've lost in a week was $10,000. Despite the large numbers, I've never been late with a payment, nor has Johnny.

It was surprisingly easy losing $100,000. My problem was that I won too much too quickly. The winning streak made me feel invincible. $40,000 no longer seemed good enough for me. I wanted to be up $80,000. From there, I got reckless. My gut said to go with the Atlanta Falcons on Sunday morning, and that was all I needed to hear. I let it ride. I put everything on the Falcons to win by three points or more.

The Falcons won by two, and I lost. I should have taken that as a sign and quit, but I didn't. I couldn't. There were more football games to be played. The New York Giants were playing in primetime on "Sunday Night Football." Plus, in my eyes, despite losing $40,000 rather quickly, I was still even. I called Johnny and told him I wanted $25,000 on the New York Giants.

This was a big mistake. Instead of going back to $500 bets, building up a profit, and then gambling large, I went for the gusto right off the bat. I got greedy. After being up so much earlier that day, $500 seemed like chump change. I wanted that invincibility back. But this wasn't a smart bet. I had done no research on the game. I simply felt the vibe of the fans walking around my new city with their Giants gear on. I went with it.

The Giants lost, and I was down $25,000. My heart dropped. At this point, I was already in over my head. I had no choice but to roll the dice again. Monday rolled around, which meant "Monday Night Football." I called Johnny and told him I wanted $25,000 on the Dallas Cowboys. I felt good about the pick. The Cowboys are known as America's team. Last time I checked, I'm American. The red, white and blue would bail me out. They had to, right?

Wrong again. I was down $50,000. I made one last call to Johnny. There was a late night basketball game on the west coast. The Los Angeles Lakers were playing the Knicks in L.A. I told him I wanted one more bet before I paid up. A newfound hatred for New York sport teams now burned inside of me, so I told him that I wanted $50,000 on the Lakers. I assured Johnny that I was good for it. He had no clue that I was technically unemployed. He was slightly hesitant, but ultimately, he let me place the bet. In the long run, it didn't matter if I was good for it or not. I placed the bet, so if I lost, I'd be paying him in one-way or another.

All the Lakers needed to do was win by four points. At home, against the Knicks, that was a no-brainer. With 10 seconds left, the Lakers were up by six points. With 9 seconds left, a premonition crept over me. I sat down, laid my head back and closed my eyes. The announcers took it from there.

"This one is in the books, Jim. The nail is in the coffin. Lakers grab the win at home!"

"It certainly looks that way, Bob."

"Smith throws up a deep three, and it's good!"

"Lakers lead is cut to three. I'm afraid it's a little too little, too late, though, Bob."

"Right you are, Jim. Lakers throw it deep to Young! He's got a wide-open dunk! Five, four, and Young dribbles it back out. He's going to smartly run this clock out. That's a veteran play, Jim."

"Indeed it was, Bob. And the Lakers are going to escape with a three point victory."

I wanted to let Jim and Bob know how much I truly, truly despised them. I took a deep breath, and then I completely panicked. The first thought I had was to get in my car and drive. I'd never return to New York again. That thought was quickly interrupted by an incoming call on my cell phone. It was Johnny. Fuck.

"Beau-diddly! Rough day. How about those Lakers?"

I could feel his smile through the phone, and I hated it.

"Brutal," I said.

"I know, Beau...I know. I almost felt bad for you, but then I remembered I was about to get 100 large, so I cheered up! When can you have my money ready?"

"Funny you should ask, Johnny, because it may take me a little while to get the full $100,00 ready."

"You know, Beau, I could've sworn you said you were good for it when you threw these bets down," he said.

"I am, eventually..."

"I'm going to cut you a *little bit* of slack, only because you've never been late on a payment before. How long is a little while for you?"

"Eh, I don't know...a few months?"

"A few months!"

"A year tops."

"Are you fucking kidding me?" Johnny shouted into the phone, "How much can you give me today?"

"Today, I'd say I could probably throw you about $10,000 cash, along with my car, which is also worth about $10,000."

"That's no good, Beau. That's no good at all. I trusted you, and you've fucked me over."

"I know, Johnny, I'm sorry, it wasn't my intent-"

"Shut the fuck up, Beau," Johnny continued. "Here's what we're going to do. First of all, that piece of shit car is not worth $10,000. We're going to call it $5,000. You've got $10,000 in cash. So you can do $15,000 today. You still owe $85,000. You'll have 5% interest every month. What are the odds you'll be able to pay this?"

"Decent," I answered with an up-beat attitude. I couldn't believe he thought my car was worth $5,000, but I was pretty excited about it. There's no way it was actually worth more than $500 at this point.

"Dammit, Beau. That doesn't give me much confidence at all. How much do you make per month?"

"Depends on how hot I get," I said.

"Not including gambling," Johnny continued. "How much do you make from your job?"

"Well," I paused. "Gambling is my job."

"You've got to be kidding me," Johnny said. "Get the $10,000 and your car and be at my grandma's house in Jersey tonight at 7. Don't make me come looking for you."

Johnny hung up the phone. I was worried, but meeting him at his grandma's house made me feel better about the whole situation. Johnny wouldn't get violent in her house. I knew his grandma. I've watched a few games with Johnny at her house. She likes me, and she's given me chocolate chip cookies every time I've been there. I hope that streak continues.

I brushed my teeth and went to use the bathroom before leaving. While I stood at the toilet contemplating my fate, I decided that I should call my own Grandma, Winnie, before leaving - just in case. We speak on the phone *every* Tuesday, and I didn't want $100,000 of debt to the mafia to stop that.

I reached into my pocket for my phone, but when I pulled it out, it slipped, and fell directly into the toilet. It was the last straw. I was furious. I was up $40,000 yesterday. It would have been so easy to buy a new phone if I had cashed out. I would do terrible things to rewind the clock, just this once, to early Sunday morning. I stared at the phone, which was now sitting in a pool of urine. The money and the mafia may not have been able to stop me from calling Winnie, but a urine-covered phone most certainly could. I grabbed my keys, drove to the bank, withdrew the $10,000 I had to my name, and mentally prepared myself for a trip to New Jersey.

Chapter III

LET THE BIG DOG EAT

"You've got to be kidding me," Johnny said. "Get the $10,000 and your car and be at my grandma's house in Jersey tonight at 7. Don't make me come looking for you." Johnny hung up the phone and walked back to the tee box of Meadow Creek Golf Club's first hole.

"Who was that?" Arno asked.

"This fucking guy is down 100 large and he doesn't have it."

"What his asset situation look like?"

"He's not even close."

"You let this guy bet 100K without knowing his situation? What were you thinking?" Arno asked.

"I don't know. You're right. I just kind of trusted him, I guess," Johnny said.

"You what?"

"I trusted him."

"Why the fuck would you trust *anybody* outside of the family?"

"I don't know – there's just something about this guy. He's-"

"Do you know how vulnerable that not only makes you, but the entire family? *Never* trust anybody outside of the family," Arno sternly interrupted.

Arno's been the boss of his New York mafia family for the past 20 years and counting. He rose to the top of La Cosa Nostra by trusting his gut and acting swiftly. If he even suspects that someone in his organization is a rat, that person gets disposed of. His gut is normally right, and to this point, it's kept nearly all of his men out of prison. They love and respect him for it.

Recently, however, Arno has been slipping. He feels that his time is almost up. The man who had always laughed at the idea of fear is now worried, and for no particular reason. He's started to suspect everyone of being a rat – which has caused him to distance himself from the family. They've noticed.

The one man determined to get Arno out of his funk is Johnny. Johnny would, most likely, be the man to sit on the throne *if* Arno were to go down. Despite his potential promotion, Johnny wants to help Arno. Arno has never been anything but fair to Johnny. He owes it to him to return the favor. He's been trying for weeks to get Arno back on the streets, but the only thing Arno ever comes out of his house for is a round of golf. So, they golf.

"You're right, you're right," Johnny continued. "It won't happen again."

"Good. So what's your plan for this guy?" Arno asked.

"Well, by tonight, I'll know if he'll *ever* be able to pay, that's for sure. If he can't, I'll get to have a little fun, I suppose. Do you want to join?"

"No, no," Arno continued as he took a few practice swings. "I've got dinner with the wife and kids tonight."

"I'll take care of it," Johnny said.

"I believe you, "Arno answered. "Do you know why I believe you?"

"Because we're family," Johnny said.

"Exactly, Johnny. Now let's get back to the situation at hand – this par 4."

"Let the big dog eat, boss," Johnny said.

Arno stared at the ball. He imagined hitting it cleanly, long and straight, right down the middle. When his mind was clear, he swung, and mimicked his vision to perfection.

"That's what I'm talking about," Johnny congratulated. "You're getting pretty good at golf."

"I should be getting good," Arno replied. "I've been playing three times a week. I've even started reading golf magazines for tips."

"That must be what my game is missing - the magazines," Johnny continued. "Because I've been out here with you almost every round, and I still suck." Johnny took a swig of his beer, put it back in the golf cart, and walked to the tee box. He put his ball down quickly, lined up, and swung without thinking. It sailed into the trees on the right. "Dammit."

"Maybe you should try playing a round without drinking," Arno suggested.

"I don't know about that, boss," Johnny continued. "That's my favorite part about golf. I can drink and still be a respectable golfer."

"Or you could stay sober and become a good golfer."

"You may be right, but with the way you've been swinging the clubs, I wouldn't be able to beat you in any state of mind, so I might as well continue getting drunk."

"Quit kissing my ass," Arno said as they got in their golf cart. "Even though you're probably right…"

Johnny hated being on the golf course. He'd rather be on the streets, making collections. He enjoyed it. He thrived on seeing panic in the eyes of degenerate gamblers as he approached them, and he always felt like the heavyweight champion of the world after they handed him an envelope full of cash.

The pair quickly made their way through the first five holes. Arno was sitting at even par. Johnny was 3 beers deep, and 10 over par. As they approached the sixth tee box, a par 3, they noticed there was a wait. Two men were on the tee box, watching another group, who were standing just off the green.

"What's the deal here?" Arno asked the men, whose backs were turned towards him. They turned around and answered.

"Arno! What's up, big guy?" A young man asked.

"Ayyy! Extreme Boyd! How's it hanging?" Arno responded.

"A little to the left, as always," he answered. "Arno, I want you to meet my new assistant attorney. He's sharp as a tack. He'll be an asset for us. This is my protégé, Drew Riley."

"How you doin'?" Arno asked Drew as he shook his hand.

"It's an honor to meet you," Drew responded.

"Johnny, have you ever met Taylor Boyd? He's been my attorney for the past 3 years."

"Thankfully, I haven't," Johnny continued. "No offense, but the less I deal with lawyers, the better business is for me. How you doin', Taylor?"

"I can't argue with that," Taylor answered as he shook Johnny's hand. "If you *do* ever need a lawyer, though, I'll beat whatever charge they throw at you. I own the D.A. in court."

"He's right," Arno said. "He got the PeNabs off of their most recent assault charges. When the judge read the 'not guilty' verdict, the prosecutor went nuts. It was the first time I've seen a prosecutor get held in contempt of court."

"The prosecutors can blow me. I'm just interested in defending my good people of New York," Taylor said.

"I like this guy, boss," Johnny said. "Just out of curiosity, how old are you? You look pretty young."

"I appreciate that," Taylor responded. "I'm 30."

"How'd you become a top lawyer so fast?" Johnny asked.

"Do you remember when Leo de Luca got pinched three years back, and then his lawyer got ripped a new asshole by the prosecutor?" Arno asked Johnny.

"Of course. He got 30 years. It's a damn shame," Johnny answered.

"Well, after the trial, Taylor walked up to me and told me that if he had been Leo's lawyer, Leo would've walked free that very day. I liked his confidence, and I hired him on the spot. Since then, the very few times our friends have been to court, Taylor has won for us. He's quickly becoming a friend of ours."

"Thanks, Arno," Taylor said.

"Well, it's good to meet ya', Taylor," Johnny said.

"Likewise," he responded.

"So what's the deal here? Why are we waiting around?" Arno asked Taylor.

"I don't know. These fucking guys in front of us have been taking forever. We caught up to them last hole. We've had to wait about 20 minutes in between every shot since. They haven't offered to let us play through, either."

"Motherfuckers with no golf etiquette. It pisses me off so bad. They're probably terrible, too."

"That would be an understatement," Taylor said.

"Goddammit," Arno said. "HEY! MOTHERFUCKERS! MOVE YOUR ASS!"

"Nice," Taylor said.

The four men on the green turned around and starred. One of them had the audacity to cup his hand around his ear, motioning for Arno to repeat himself.

"Son of a bitch," Arno said as he teed his ball up.

"Are you playing into them?" Taylor asked.

"Yep," he replied.

Arno swung his 5-iron, and sent the ball sailing right for the group. Three of the men covered their heads and scattered in separate directions. The fourth was oblivious, and stayed where he was.

"That's on line," Taylor said.

"It's artwork," Arno replied, still striking a pose.

The man stood still, seemingly in disbelief that Arno had played into him. When he realized the shot was heading for him, he tried to run, but it was too late. Hit drilled him in the back, and he fell to the green.

"No way!" Johnny said.

"Well, let's get the fuck out of here," Arno told Johnny.

"Good call," Johnny answered.

"Taylor, I assume you and Drew can handle this?

"Of course," Taylor replied.

"Perfect. I'll be in touch if I need you," Arno said.

"Have a good one," Taylor said.

Arno and Johnny hoped in their golf cart and headed back to Johnny's car. When they arrived, they tossed their clubs in the trunk and left. Before Johnny dropped Arno off, he took one last stab at sparking his interest in a little mafia family time.

"So, boss man," Johnny said.

"What's up?

"Are you sure you don't want to join tonight? It could be fun."

"I'm sure will be," Arno said. "But the Baked ziti is calling my name."

"You haven't really joined in on any of the fun recently. Are you okay?" Johnny asked.

"Don't' worry about me, Johnny. I'm fine. I've got well-oiled machine rolling thanks to you and the guys. It's allowed me to play golf and have more family time. That's all."

"Okay, boss," Johnny continued, "But we'd still like to get some family time with you, too."

"Noted. Keep up the good work – starting with this asshole tonight. Fuck him up and take all of his assets. Problem solved," Arno said.

"That's the plan. The only problem is that I kind of like the guy. He's a good dude, so it's going to be rough having to do this."

"Are you kidding me? Who gives a fuck? Go get the money and/or fuck him up. Your only friends are your family. Remember that."

"You're right," Johnny continued. "You're right."

"Anything else?" Arno asked.

"Well, if you change your mind, he's going to be at my grandma's house at 7 tonight."

"I'll put it down as my Plan B," Arno said. "Remember who your friends are, Johnny. Take care of business."

"Will do, boss."

Chapter IV

THE OLD SEX GAG - PART TWO

When I pulled into the driveway of Johnny's Grandma's house, the first thing I noticed was that her Buick wasn't there. Her Buick was always there and she was always home. I had no clue that she could actually drive. I figured she kept the car in the driveway to retain a sense of her youth. 99 year-olds should not be driving. Something didn't feel right. A little old lady with chocolate chip cookies really would've lightened the mood.

I cut my car off and sat in the driver's seat for a moment. This would be the last time I would drive my car. We've had some good times together. It may be old and beat-up, but I loved it. I took a deep breath, gave a love tap to the steering wheel and exited.

I felt sick to my stomach as I walked to the front door, but I ignored my gut. I took another deep breath. Before I could knock, the door swung open. In front of me stood two very large identical twins. They were the biggest twins I had ever seen. They must have been at least 6'6" and weighed 250 a piece. They both had jet-black hair that was pulled back into a ponytail. When I glanced at their attire, I realized I was fucked. They were both dressed in all black, and they were wearing plastic gloves. Plastic gloves? What the fuck were those for? I glanced back towards my car. My instincts were screaming, "Run!" However, there was no time for that.

They grabbed me and threw me inside. I hit the ground hard. I jumped up and tried to protect my self, but, as it turns out, the brown belt I received in karate when I was a kid didn't pay off. They tackled me back to the ground in no time. I was helpless.

"What the fuck?" I yelled right before a huge fist drilled me in the face. Another fist followed into my gut, and a third broke my nose. One of their boots smashed into my rib cage. The party ended with another fist to my eye. It landed cleanly. I rolled on the floor in agony. I was yanked to my feet. My arms were pinned behind my back. They dragged me down a hallway and opened a door. It led to the basement. They tossed me down the flight of stairs. I tried to stand, but a boot re-connected with my ribs. One of the giants ripped my shirt off. Next, he pulled off my shoes, followed by my pants, and finished by removing my boxers. They grabbed a chair and tossed me into it. My arms were pulled behind the backrest and tied together. My feet were pulled back, crossed and then tied together.

I looked up at the twins, who smiled and said something in Italian to each other. Next, they slapped me across the face repetitively – 30 times or so, laughing hysterically in-between every blow. It was more insulting than painful. When they were finished having their fun, they pulled out a black bandana, folded it into a blindfold and tied it over my eyes. A few seconds later, a gag was in my mouth and tied behind my head. It tasted musky and moist. I nearly vomited while thinking about its history. At this point, the only thing I could do was hope that it was bought for this occasion, and it wasn't the one Johnny's Grandma may or may not have owned since the early 1960s. There's not much worse than having an old, used-up sex gag in your mouth.

I breathed heavily through my nose – which was dripping blood. I heard footsteps marching back up the stairs. A light-switch turned off, and the door slammed shut. This was not good.

Chapter V

BAD VIBES

Is this really how it all ends? Why didn't I just drive south? How the fuck did I end up here? My mind raced through the possibilities of my current situation. It didn't take long for it to settle on the fact that I was about to be fucking murdered. It was the first time in my life that I didn't feel invincible. Death just never seemed plausible. It was something that other people did. Surely it wouldn't happen to me until I was about 120 years old, and by then, someone will have figured out the whole "being immortal" deal.

When you feel invincible, you're able to find humor in bad situations. It's been that way for every problem that I've encountered in my life. However, I didn't find this situation very funny. At 27, I didn't envision myself being naked, tied to a chair, blindfolded and gagged with what I feared to be a 99 year-old woman's sex toy. On top of that, all of this is happening in the basement of that very 99 year-old lady's house. If you had told me that a year ago, I would have said that the worse case scenario would be that I was in an intimate relationship with her - because of her beautiful soul. I would not have seen this coming.

What kind of animal would do this in his own Grandma's house? There is a major difference between paying someone a little money at her house and being tied up in her basement. Any time you're at a Grandma's house, it should be considered "base," free from any type of murdering shenanigans. In fact, any time you're in a woman's house that is old enough to potentially be a Grandma, thugs should not be allowed to come in, tie you up and kill you. If I'm the boss of a crime family, I'm setting that rule in stone. No killing near old women, period. Even if they don't see it, it can't happen in a house that they own. Unfortunately, it doesn't look like these guys share my view on that matter. What sick fucks.

I can't believe I was a fan of the mafia before this. I always thought that I would have made a great mafia member. In fact, I think mafia-on-mafia murders should be legal. They knew what they were signing up for when they joined. As long as they don't break the rules, they'll be fine. Or at least that's how *The Godfather* and *The Sopranos* made it out to be.

I guess The Eagle does things differently. I heard that he tortures his victims before making them "disappear." I was into the story when I originally heard it from Zuber. It's not nearly as cool now that I'm the one on the receiving end. I've made a lot of extremely dumb decisions in my life with little or no consequence, and karma finally paid a visit.

I can't stop thinking about how it's going to happen. The possibilities are endless. I heard he once drained a man of his blood while he was still alive. He's also allegedly frozen people, crushed them to death and starved them to death. My favorite story is that Arno flew a guy up on his two-passenger plane and jumped out of it with a parachute, just so the other guy could die via plane crash. Apparently it was that guy's biggest fear.

I'm pretty picky about the way I want to die. First of all, I hope he makes a bone-chilling speech before he finishes me. It needs to be frightening, but also enlightening. The speech needs to help me figure out life, and accept that mine has come to an end. They say that any day you learn something new is a good day. I guess that would still apply to the day you die, right?

At the end of the speech, I think I'd prefer a bullet to the head, just one *BANG*, and it's done. But then again, people have survived gunshot wounds to the head. What if I live through it? I have zero interest in non-lethal gunshot wounds. And as much as I would like an instant death, I would also like a brief moment when I can think to myself, "So – this is how it happens." A vintage death, if you will.

Being hung upside down for a really long period of time is out of the question. I won't allow it. I hate when blood rushes to my head. I don't know if I'd die from that or not, but I know that it would be terrible. While I'm on that subject, I'm going to go ahead and rule out being hung by the neck as well. Yes, it's instant, but having to experience the feeling of falling right before it's all over simply doesn't sound appealing to me.

Being lit on fire is a pretty rare way to go out - but that might just be the worst way someone can die. No one should have to go through that, including me. The only way that any type of fire situation would be acceptable is if they give me a Viking-like funeral. That would be okay. Kill me, put the gold coins over my eyes, push me out onto the river and have someone shoot a flaming arrow onto my floating grave. That would be very stylish.

I'm not interested in creatures being involved in my death - specifically snakes, spiders or bees. Being bitten by a poisonous snake or spider just seems miserable. I'd have to sit there, convulsing, as the poison slowly worked its way through my body. Bees would be the worst out of those three. Bee stings hurt. I don't care what anyone says. They hurt, and it would take hundreds of stings to kill me. Fuck that.

Let's toss knives out of the equation as well. Paper cuts sting pretty bad, so I can't even imagine how badly it sucks to get stabbed. Every time I've been cut, I've acted like a baby. I pride myself on having a high tolerance for pain, but if I see a knife, I'll beg. I'm not too proud to beg. I see nothing wrong with it. If it's either weep on my knees while begging for mercy or be paper cut repetitively, I'll beg and weep, no questions asked.

Likewise, I refuse to have my jaw broken during this whole ordeal. I've been down that road, and it's miserable. I drank my meals through a straw for three months. I've been nervous about it re-breaking ever since. If there are any positives to take from this situation thus far, it's that my jaw held up to a few punches from the twin mobsters.

One method I'd be willing to discuss would be a beheading - going out like they did in the old days. It would have to be chopped off via guillotine, though. A guillotine is one of those old wood contraptions that have the holes for the arms and head. The blade falls from the top and slices the head off. It's almost like a cigar cutter, just one clean *SWOOSH* and it's done. That could potentially leave a cool legacy, too. It may even make national news. I'll be known as the guy who had his head cut off in a medieval cigar cutter. Now that's vintage.

No - I need to think positively. Maybe death isn't inevitable and this is all just a scare tactic. I think my best shot at getting out of this is through Johnny's Grandma. If she needs to do the laundry while these guys are away, I guarantee that I can convince her into untying me. I didn't see a washer and dryer during the brief moment I had my vision in the basement, but it's probably down here. All I need is the time it would take her to separate her light clothes from dark. I would also need a way to get this gag out of my mouth in order to convince her to untie me, though.

Wait a second, that's it! She'll see that I have her sex gag in my mouth, and she'll take it out, because, naturally, she needs it for her super active sex life. I can't help but wonder, if this is indeed her gag, what it looks like. I know she's old, which would lead to the obvious decision of a plain sex gag with black leather straps and a red rubber ball, but I kind of sense something a little more exciting. Her sex gag has a little bit more pizazz. I'm guessing it has a black rubber ball with leopard print straps. Maybe zebra print straps. Who knows?

It sounds pretty quiet upstairs, though. Maybe she died, and that's why her Buick wasn't here. That would also explain Johnny's bad mood. If she's not dead already, maybe she *will* die in the next couple of hours. She is extremely old after all. But, it would have to be a death that comes as a shock, so the family goes into mourning for longer than usual.

That would be a tall order. Her family has probably expected her death for a few years now. BUT, if she were to die in a vicious manner, Arno would feel badly because he was conducting business in her house when she died. He'd order an immediate halt to all business, and he'd release me while forgiving all of my debts. It would have to be one seriously fucked up death for that to happen.

A bad car accident might do, as long as the jaws of life are necessary to get her out of the car. A sky diving accident could work, too. Maybe her parachute doesn't open, she falls 10,000 feet into a thorn bush, but doesn't die. No one ever finds her. Every millimeter she moves stings with pain – but it doesn't kill her. She eventually dies from not having drinking water. If either of those death options pan out, I might be in business.

Wait - what am I thinking? I shouldn't wish that kind of evil on anyone, not even on Johnny, or his Grandma. For the record, I hope Johnny's Grandma lives to be over 100, and the *NBC Today Show* gives her a brief moment on national television with her face on the *Smucker's* jar. That would be nice for her.

Also – now that I think about it, being murdered by the mafia would leave a cooler legacy than I've currently left for myself. If the mafia doesn't kill me, I'd be just another guy with two first names. On the flip side, if they do kill me, I'd be interesting. The inevitable future documentary on Arno would give me my five minutes of fame. They'll ask, "Who the hell was that dead guy?"

You know what? That sounds okay to me. I'm tired of being a fuck up, and even more so, I'm tired of being tired. Nothing ever worked out like I thought it would, but this might. This way, I'll go out with a bang.

Chapter VI

SLICED AND DICED

I awoke to the sound of a door slamming shut. It took me a few seconds to realize where I was. I heard footsteps moving upstairs. I wanted it to be Johnny's Grandma, but it wasn't. There were too many footsteps and each landed with a thud. Panic crept back in. I took a few deep breaths and tried to calm myself down.

There were only two rules that I had lived my life by up to this point. First, find humor in every moment possible. I love laughing. I wake up with sore cheeks from chuckling on a daily basis. It's simply a necessity. Second, don't be a little bitch. What I mean by that is someone who is extremely egotistical, constantly complaining about something, and is always in a pretty bad mood. Most of the time, a little bitch will be rude in restaurants, leave small tips and chew with their mouths open. They're just awful. It's very important to not be a little bitch.

I decided right then and there that there was no need to break my two rules just as I'm about to die. If I'm going to go out, I should go out with dignity. No whining. No crying. Get a last laugh in if possible. If this is how it ends, then this is how it ends. I felt calm.

The basement door swung open and banged against the wall. It sounded like a stampede of men rushing down the stairs. After each person stepped from the last wood step, which creaked loudly, to the concrete floor, the room fell silent. That silence was frightening. I could feel them around me. I was actually happy when one of them violently yanked off my blindfold. It was Johnny and the two identical goons.

"Beau! Whatayya know whatayya say?" Johnny blurted out.

"I hope your Grandma breaks her hip," I said into the gag. Luckily, there was no chance that anyone could make those words out.

"What's that, Beau? I didn't quite understand," Johnny mocked.

"I said that I hope you accidentally see your grandma naked, spread eagle one day."

"Oh, that's right, you can't talk with a gag in your mouth."

One of the giant twins walked over and unbuckled my sex-slave gag. What do you know? It was as plain as could be. There were no animal print straps to be found. It was simply black leather straps with the red rubber ball. Johnny's grandma kept it classy.

"What the fuck, Johnny? Why are you being such an asshole?" I questioned. "I thought we were friends, man."

"Friends?"

"Yeah, dude, friends. I've been down here thinking about how I hope your Grandma lives to be 100, and the *Today Show* puts her face on a *Smucker's* jar on national fucking television. Would a non-friend be having those thoughts? I don't think so."

"What the fuck did you say to me?" Johnny asked.

"How could you possibly take any offense to that? I said I hope your Grandma lives to be 100, and the *Today Show* puts her face on a *Smucker's* jar."

"You want my Grandma's face on a jar?"

"You've never seen the *Today Show* segment where they put 100 year-old people's faces on a jar of *Smucker's* and give them a few moments on national television?"

As he stared blankly into my eyes, I realized that he had not.

"The *Smucker's* jar segment on the *Today Show* is a hit. If a person lives to be 100, they should get their face on the *Smucker's* jar on national television," I ranted.

"Can you believe this fuckin' guy?" Johnny asked one of the monstrous twins. He shook his head from side to side. I would hate to have an identical twin. I know a few sets of identical twins, and they're awesome. But, it's not for me. It would freak me out to see someone who looks just like me. One solid advantage that an identical twin gives is being able to really see how your outfit for the day will look by having the other twin try it on first. Mirrors would be completely unnecessary.

"Do you not feel a little weird about doing this in your Grandma's house, Johnny?" I asked. "It's pretty fucked up. I was just thinking that there should be a rule against killing people near Grandma's. Especially in their house!"

"You obviously don't know my Grandma. My Grandma was married to my Grandfather, Anthony Santoro," Johnny said with a twisted smirk.

"I've never heard of him," I said.

"Exactly. He kept his name out of the papers. He was successful. That's more than you'll ever dream about doing with your life."

"I'm not so sure about that. I dream about being a billionaire, traveling the world in private jets, surrounded by super models, four to five nights a week."

He stared at me for a moment, before cracking a smile and shaking his head from side to side.

"Can I ask one question?"

"One," Johnny replied.

"Why is there a sex-gag in your Grandma's house?"

"We brought it from the strip club for you. The strippers use them on a nightly basis. After a very long career, that hand-me-down of a sex gag was just retired."

"Ugh, dude. Sick. That is fucked up. I would have preferred it to be your Grandma's."

That statement awarded me the backside of Johnny's hand. The identical goons walked over to me and dropped a book bag next to my feet. They both knelt as one of them unzipped the bag and took out a packet of paper.

"What's that for?"

"Paper cuts," Johnny answered.

"Get out of here. Seriously, what's that for?"

"Fuck you, Beau," Johnny went on, "I've had to listen to your bit on paper cuts a thousand times. Nearly every time you have a couple of drinks. It's your 'go to' joke. When you're drunk and you're about to lose a bet, you open it up with a remark about how you're being tortured, and then you move into the spiel on paper cuts. You've told me all about hanging upside down, the bit about the knives, about being shot non-lethally, the part on how snakes, spiders, and bees, and your fear of being set on fire, too. I'm so tired of hearing it that I'm going to start telling it. You're going to hear it, and experience it. It's going to suck."

"You're going to use my 'go to' against me?"

"I'm going to use your 'go to' against you," Johnny vowed.

"Fuck."

"That's right," Johnny continued. "Bitch."

"You have no creativity," I said.

"Fuck you, Beau. I don't want any creativity for this. I want you to experience exactly what you don't want to experience. Do you know why?"

"Why?"

"Because you made me look bad - really bad. I'm in a business where being made to look bad isn't good for business. I'm down $100,000 because you can't pay. That means my boss is down $100,000. He's going to want that money. If we can't get it, then you're going to pay in blood money. It's as simple as that."

"Goddammit," I blurted.

"Probably not the best time to be taking the Lord's name in vein, Beau," Johnny responded.

"Oh, no? You don't think so?" I questioned. "You think the Lord is cool with the way you're currently acting?"

"Natural selection," Johnny answered.

"Do you even know what that means?" I asked. The question awarded me with another back-handed slap.

"Okay - you're right," I said. "This is natural selection."

"Smart man, Beau. I'd rather get started with this paper on skin action, anyway. Like I said, you've given me the game plan. Now, I'm going to execute it."

There was nothing I could say. He won. The goons each grabbed a foot. I kicked furiously until Johnny pulled out a knife and pressed it firmly against my naked testicles.

I froze in fear.

"Whew! Cold!" I joked.

"You're going to sit there and get paper-cut or I'm going to slice your nuts off. Your call," Johnny threatened.

"I'll take the paper," I stuttered.

"Good decision," Johnny said.

The goons went back to work. They began with the space between my big toe and second toe.

"Do it, PeNabs," Johnny ordered. Both men prepared for action.

"Both of your names are PeNab?" I asked.

"We call them both PeNab. Their actual names are Tommy and Geno," Johnny said.

"Tommy and Geno? How do you get PeNab out of that?"

"I have no clue," Johnny continued. "We call them both PeNab because they're identical, and they do every single job together. It's easier. They don't give a shit what we call them anyway. They just like getting paid to rough people up. As you'll see, they're good at their jobs."

The PeNabs continued. They put a piece of paper in between the big toe and second toe and looked straight at each other.

"Wait, wait, wait!" I yelled.

"Fuck you, Beau. Do it, PeNabs."

"Uno...due...tre!" They shouted in Italian.

On "tre," the PeNabs slid their paper deep into my skin. After a split second of no pain, it settled in, and it felt like my toes were on fire. I bit my lower lip and grunted in agony. Geno and Tommy laughed and high-fived each other.

"You sick fucks!" I screamed.

They laughed, and then moved to the gap between my second and third toes.

"I hate you both," I informed them.

"Uno...due...tre!" They repeated with an equal amount of joy.

Once again, the paper was slid down quickly, and pain settled in. I screamed in distress.

"Hey now," Johnny started. "My Grandma is asleep. You don't want to wake up a little old lady, do you? Plus, this is just round one - the paper cut round. If you're going to scream like that, I'm going to put the gag back in, but I'm pretty sure I already see a cold sore forming. Your choice."

"Ahhhhhhh," I yelled in frustration. "I'll be quiet. I exaggerated a bit on the last one, anyway. I was actually trying to get your Grandma's attention."

"My Grandma would come down here and help if I asked her to. Get that through your head," Johnny said as he lightly smacked me in the face a few times.

The urge to insult his Grandma boiled inside me. However, because I was trying to keep the paper cuts to a minimum, I stayed quiet. Geno and Tommy went down the line of toes, paper cutting each with fury. I could feel blood trickling down the bottom of my feet. My worst nightmare was coming true.

"Enough! This is fucking ridiculous," I yelled. When they were done with the gaps in between my toes, they decided to paper cut horizontally at the bottom of my toes and where the joints bend.

"Wait, PeNabs!" Johnny yelled. "Beau thinks this is ridiculous. Let's call if off and go home."

The PeNabs stopped and looked at him. The serious look on Johnny's face quickly disappeared, and the three erupted into laughter.

"I'm just kidding! Keep it rolling!"

With each stinging paper cut, I thought more about karma. I hope it exists. I want instant karma. I want each of these assholes to receive paper cuts identical to my own.

"Johnny, just kill me. I don't care anymore."

"No," he replied.

"You're such an asshole," I said.

"What'd you call me?"

"I called you an asshole. You don't have the balls to shoot me in the head right now."

"PeNabs, hold off a second," Johnny said. The moved aside, and he stood in front of me. He began to breathe heavier and heavier, and finally, he snapped. He threw haymakers, one after another, into my rib cage. I tightened my stomach as much as possible to absorb the blows, but it didn't take long before I had lost my breath, and was in a serious struggle to breathe.

"Goddamn that felt good!"

I coughed and gasped for air.

"PeNab, hand me my knife," Johnny said.

One of the PeNabs handed him an absurdly large knife. He pressed his finger to the point of the knife to test the sharpness.

"Do you like my knife, Beau?"

"It's a bit excessive. I assume that's because you're trying to make up for something," I said.

Johnny chuckled, "I'm going to enjoy this."

"You're a little bitch. The PeNabs are little bitches. Arno is probably the biggest little bitch of all."

"You know what," Johnny paused while he stared at me. "I need to make a call. I'll be right back."

Chapter VII

JUST WHAT THE DOCTOR ORDERED

"Hey, Arno," Johnny said.

"What do you need, Johnny? I'm eating."

"Sorry about that, I'll make it quick," he continued. "Do you remember that thing we were talking about earlier?"

"Yeah. What about it?" Arno asked.

"Well, it's not really going as planned. To be honest, I'm a little confused, and I could use a little guidance."

Arno sighed. "There's nothing confusing about it. You either figure out a way for it to continue, or you end it."

"That's the thing," Johnny continued. "He wants me to end it."

"What do you mean, 'he wants you to end it.' Everybody always wants to continue it."

"Not this guy. He's not being very nice about it either. He wants me to end it."

"That's what he said?" Arno asked.

"That's what he said," Johnny answered.

"What an asshole," Arno said.

"So, what do you think? Should I end it and be done with it, or should I try to figure something else out?" Johnny asked.

Arno took another deep breath out of frustration. "Goddammit."

"What's the problem?" Johnny asked.

"It's baked ziti night, that's the problem. I was planning on enjoying this lovely dish and then putting on sweatpants. I didn't anticipate having to deal with this shit," Arno said.

"Listen, don't even worry about it. I just thought you should know that he called me and the PeNabs little bitches."

"He did?" Arno asked. "Well - that takes some balls."

"He called you the biggest little bitch of all," Johnny said.

"I'll be right over," Arno replied.

"You're coming over?" Johnny asked.

"I'll be there in 30 minutes."

"Perfect. See ya' in a few," Johnny said.

Chapter VIII

THE EAGLE

BAM!

The basement door swung open. Johnny walked back down.

"That was Arno. He's on his way over," Johnny said.

"Arno?" One of the PeNabs asked.

"That's right," Johnny continued. "It turns out Beau's reckless attitude intrigued him. Thanks, Beau."

"The Eagle is coming here?" I asked.

"The Eagle? I thought he was the biggest little bitch of all?"

"Did I say that?"

"God, I'm going to enjoy this. Arno hasn't done much of the dirty work recently. I have a feeling he may be coming back with a vengeance."

"What's he been doing instead?" I asked.

"Golfing," Johnny answered.

"He's a mob boss and a golfer? That's pretty rad," I said.

"He's a really good golfer, actually," Johnny continued. "Now shut the fuck up. Let's get started without him. He'll be here soon enough."

Johnny grabbed his knife and walked over towards me. He dug his blade gently into my stomach, at the bottom of the right side of my rib cage. The blade broke the skin, and blood trickled down. He didn't cut deep, but it was excruciatingly painful. I winced as he then traced the knife up my stomach, over my belly button and down to the bottom of my left rib cage. With my nipples included, my torso now looked like a sad face. How appropriate. Blood began to flow faster. My stomach felt like it was on fire. It was so painful that I had no choice but to erupt into laughter. It had always been my way of dealing with extreme pain. It took Johnny by surprise.

"Are you seriously fucking laughing?" Johnny asked.

"I can't help it," I said between laughs.

The PeNabs slowly began to chuckle, and then they erupted into a laughing attack as well. Johnny looked up at them, and smirked. The smirk turned into the gigs. The gigs turned into tears of laughter. Just four dudes, laughing and crying it out over a little torture.

The door swung open and a man trotted down the steps. It was Arno - The Eagle. He was dressed in a custom-tailored black suit. He was bald up top, but had slicked-back silver hair on the sides and back of his head. A thick mustache full of silver hair rested on his upper lip. A gold chain dangled from his neck. He was chewing on a large cigar and staring right at me. He had serious style.

The men stopped, stood up, and faced him. The chuckles faded.

"Ayyyyyy, Arno!" Johnny yelled before he hugged and kissed Arno on both cheeks.

"Boss man!" A PeNab stated in broken English before they both went in for hugs and kisses.

"What's so funny?" Arno asked.

"The sad face on my stomach," I replied.

Arno stared at me. "So, this is the guy with the deep but empty pockets, eh Johnny?"

"This is the one, boss."

"I heard you called me the biggest little bitch of all," Arno said.

"Yeah, I did. That was my bad. I was just trying to get under Johnny's skin."

Arno walked slowly over to me and looked over my face as if he were studying it.

"Nice mustache," Arno said

"Thanks, you too," I replied.

I've been able to grow a great mustache for the last 10 years. At first, I would only rock a lip sweater for a day, just to make my friends laugh. By the time I was 22, there was no more laughing. It was bold. Each whisker was jet-black. It could be spotted from 100 yards away.

Arno turned his attention to the floor around me. There were pieces of paper with blood on them everywhere.

"What's with all of this paper? Johnny, are you doing your paper cut bit on this guy?"

"What? Wait a second," I interrupted. "Johnny's paper cut bit? Johnny, I thought you hated my paper cut bit. Now, not only are you stealing the bit and literally using it against me, but you're also claiming it as your own?"

"Johnny, is this guy serious?" Arno laughed. "I've heard you tell that story a thousand times. I thought it was your one 'go to' joke."

"It's my 'go to' joke, dammit," I claimed. "Give credit where credit is due, Johnny. This is the second time you've backstabbed me today."

"I backstabbed you?" Johnny yelled.

"You front-stabbed me too, you asshole," I said.

"You bet $100,000 that you didn't have. You backstabbed me."

"Enough!" Arno said. "Next order of business. Johnny, why is this guy naked?"

"Humiliation," he answered.

"Eh, I'm not a fan. We could have done this whole routine while he was wearing shorts, no?"

"Yeah, we probably could have," Johnny answered.

"Perfect," Arno continued, "I mean, personally, I'd rather not stare at a penis while I'm working, but maybe that's just me."

"I hear you, boss," Johnny said.

"And another question," Arno continued. "Why are we using your grandma's basement for this?"

"I just figured this way if we got hungry we could run upstairs and grab a sandwich or something, ya' know?"

"Well, that's a pretty good point," Arno paused. "But, we still should have done this elsewhere. I know your Grandma has seen things in her life, but out of respect for her age and a life well-lived, she doesn't need this going on near her, much less in her own house!"

"I'm sorry, Arno, you're right. It's just that I knew I could get Beau over here without him getting suspicious," Johnny continued. "Plus, I told you about the plan for my grandma's house while we were on the golf course."

"I guess I wasn't listening very well," Arno continued. "I'm sorry."

"I'm impressed," I conceded.

"Shut the fuck up!" Arno barked in my face. "Now, back to you, Johnny. I know your intentions were good, but your Grandma is nearing 100 years old. Do you want a gunshot to go off and give her a heart attack? Think about it. Your Grandma has a legitimate opportunity to have the *Today Show* put her face on a *Smucker's* jar. That's never happened to any Grandma in this family, and you should take pride in that."

"Get the fuck out of here," I said without thinking. "I literally told him the *exact* same thing before you got---"

Before I could finish, the back of Arno's hand had bitch slapped me. His palm immediately followed across my other cheek. Luckily, my cheeks were already number, and I was getting used to it.

"Shut the fuck up," Arno yelled. "Now, Johnny, I'm just trying to say, think things through a little bit more. Having said that, now that he's here, what to do with him..."

"Maybe we should do a round of beers and discuss it," I suggested.

"I've got a better idea," Arno said. He leaned over and whispered into Johnny's ear. Johnny smiled, got up, and ran upstairs. Arno stayed, staring at me while he waited.

Johnny ran back downstairs with a grin on his face. In his left hand was a pink razor. In his right - a can of shaving cream.

"What the fuck is that for?" I questioned.

"That mustache," Arno told me. "Any man who can't afford to pay his debts shouldn't be allowed the luxury of having a mustache."

This remark cut deeper than any piece of paper would dare to dream.

"Fuck you," I said before I spit at his feet.

The PeNabs grabbed my face and held it still. Arno walked over to a sink and got a cup of water. He then lathered up my mustache, being surprisingly careful. I could tell that he truly respected mustaches, but I still rejected his opinion of my worthiness to obtain one. The first stroke from the razor might as well have sliced off a limb. Pieces of my heart swiftly fell to the ground with each strand of hair. Stroke by stroke, the reality that I would soon meet death grew. Every time I hit rock bottom in my earlier years, I looked in the mirror and said, "At least I can grow a great mustache." It's been a source of confidence. I would've liked meeting my end with that confidence on my side.

"Are you weeping?" Arno asked me.

"I wear my heart on my sleeve, and that was the meanest thing anyone has ever said to me."

When Arno was finished shaving my face, he slid a large knife from his pocket. "Listen, I've heard what I now know to be your worst nightmare routine. Shaving your mustache is not fucked up. When I light you on fire, that's when you should weep."

"That's overboard," I said.

"You don't know what the fuck you're talking about," Arno replied. "Now, Johnny, did you call Dr. Gray?"

"I did," Johnny replied. "He should be here momentarily."

"Perfect," Arno said.

A minute later, the basement door opened, and a man walked down.

"Doc!" Arno greeted.

He was carrying a black briefcase. He pulled up a chair and sat in front of me. He opened his kit. I wondered what form of torture was next. To my surprise, it was actually a medical kit. I was confused.

"Beau, this is Dr. Gray. Much like yourself, he owes us a few favors, so he's going to stitch you right up. We've got to make sure you don't die. The party must go on," Johnny informed. "For a while..."

I looked down and noticed the blood running down my thighs and completely painting my penis red. I felt a prick as Dr. Gray put an anesthetic shot in my arm. I started to lose consciousness as the doctor reached to my side and pulled a lever that reclined the chair.

"A recliner? Nice!"

I chuckled at how deep my voice sounded. I looked at my blood-covered torso and manhood again.

"Déjà vu," I mumbled as I lost consciousness.

Chapter VIV

TENTACLES AND TESTICLES

I woke up in a dark and empty room. Someone put my boxers on. It gave me a bit of dignity back while making me feel violated at the same time. It didn't take long for me to lose track of time. I tried to fall back asleep, because there is absolutely nothing else to do when you're tied to a chair. Unfortunately, sleeping while tied to a chair is not easy, especially for me. On normal night, when I sleep in a bed, I roll around – a lot. I like to alternate from sleeping on my left side, to my stomach, and then to my right side. Rise, wash, repeat. This was not possible in a chair. After I woke up for the 10th time or so, I was aggravated. I wanted to be comfortable, and that wasn't possible.

Every once in a while I'd have a visitor. The doctor came down and checked on the 30 stitches in my stomach. Johnny and/or the PeNabs occasionally came down and stuffed a ham and cheese sandwich in my face. They put a backpack with water and a tube to drink from on my lap, which was great.

However, after three visits, I was frustrated with the meal choice. There wasn't enough variety – or any for that matter. It was ham and cheese every single time. There was no mayo, no nothing. It was too dry. I could really go for anything different. Turkey and cheese would be incredible, or roast beef. Roast beef is the mafia boss of sandwich meats in my eyes. If someone would just go ahead and combine roast beef, turkey and ham for me, along with some mayo, lettuce, tomato, onions, maybe a little spicy mustard and salt and pepper - that would be great. Oh, and a good beer would be just super as well.

Realistically, though, that's probably not going to happen, so I'll scale back on my dream. I'd settle for turkey and cheese or roast beef and cheese. Anything and cheese would be better than ham and cheese. Except for bologna. Bologna sucks. It's not the taste that puts bologna at the bottom of the totem pole of lunchmeats. It's the spelling. I don't understand how the spelling and pronunciation can be so drastically different. I don't trust it. I pronounce it bo-log-na, just to stick it to the man. Ba-lone-e just doesn't make any sense.

BAM!

I know I just ranted, but I'm hoping that it's time for another ham and cheese. I'm starving. Today, after I eat, I'm going to request something different for my next meal. If I request it before, Johnny would probably go on a power trip and not give me the sandwich at all.

The lights flicked on. Arno and Johnny walked down the stairs. This was either going to be bad or terrible.

"Beau-diddly!" Johnny greeted.

"Is that my new nickname?" I questioned.

"Yeah, why not? It's fun to say," Johnny replied.

"Think of all the fun you could have saying it for the rest of your life if you don't kill me and let me go..."

"It's not that much fun to say," Arno said.

"It was worth a shot," I continued, "So, what can I do for you two gentlemen today."

"Don't be a smart ass," Johnny said.

"I see you're in your normal bright and perky mood, Johnny."

"I can't wait to bury you, Beau. You've been nothing but a thorn in my side."

"I've also been your source of jokes, apparently, don't forget that part."

"I can't even hang out at my Grandma's house in peace anymore knowing you're in the basement."

"You mean to tell me that you've been hanging out upstairs while I just sit down here all alone?" I questioned. "You should come hang out! I've never been more bored than I have been sitting down here in the dark."

"Fuck you," he answered.

"I guess the saying that you shouldn't let money get involved with friends was spot on," I replied.

"Will you two quit your bitching?" Arno demanded. "Now, Beau, I have a question about what you muttered right before you passed out from the anesthetic. Do you remember what you said?"

"My memory is terrible, Arno. In most cases, I can't remember what I had for lunch the previous day. Except in this case, however, where I'd be willing to bet my life that it was a ham and cheese sandwich."

"What?" Arno questioned. "That's not what I asked. Do you remember what you said before you passed out?"

"No."

"You said, "Déjà vu.""

"Did I?"

"You didn't have a scar from a knife on your stomach, so what's the meaning of your déjà vu?" Johnny questioned.

"Why do you give a shit, Johnny? Are you running low on stories of your own again?" I asked.

Johnny stood up with his fist raised, but Arno interrupted him.

"Ayyyyyyyy! Sit down," Arno told Johnny. "Now, Beau, answer Johnny's question. What'd you mean when you said, "Déjà vu"?"

"Why does it matter so much?"

"Because Arno said it fucking matters," Johnny barked.

"I've had a few instances of déjà vu recently, and I've been curious about the meaning behind it," Arno said. "Maybe your experience will help me put mine into perspective."

"Well, when you put it like that, Arno," I said as I glanced at Johnny, "I'll gladly tell you. I had a moment of déjà vu before I fell asleep. It was from a night in college."

"Were you tied to a chair and being tortured?" Arno asked.

"No," I continued. "I was in the streets of Key West, naked and painted like an octopus."

They both stared at me, completely confused.

"Let's have some details," Arno said, "I want to hear the story."

"What's in it for me?" I asked.

"I'll make you a deal. I'll let you live for as long as you can keep me entertained," Arno replied.

"That's not a bad deal," I continued. "I've got a few stories you might be interested in. I'll accept your deal on two conditions."

"You're not really in the bargaining position," Arno said.

I ignored him and kept my offer rolling, "First, if I agree, can I get a turkey and cheese sandwich tomorrow, with some mayo on it, and maybe a beer?" I asked him.

"Once again, if you agree, I'll let you live longer than I had originally planned. How's that sound?" Arno answered.

"Well, that doesn't sound terrible, but seeing as that it only buys me an extra day or two, and doesn't change the final outcome - I think I'd prefer the turkey and cheese, with a little mayo and a good beer," I confessed.

Arno shook his head in disbelief.

"Have it your way, Beau. Turkey and cheese with a beer for you tomorrow."

"Tomorrow?" I questioned. "How about tonight? It'd be a nice little reward after story time."

"It's already tonight," Johnny said.

"It's night time right now?" I asked in disbelief.

"Yeah, why?" Arno questioned.

"I don't know, it just felt like the morning to me. Weird."

"Well, I'll get you the sandwich and beer in the morning," Arno said.

"In the morning? Who eats sandwiches in the morning? That's more of a night time meal, is it not?"

"This guy is unbelievable," Arno said to Johnny.

"I told you boss," Johnny replied. "He just doesn't get it. Beau, you need to be lucky that we're going to give you anything to eat at all. If it were up to me, you wouldn't get a sandwich. There are people who are going to live for more than a few days that need that sandwich. Giving it to you is a waste."

"I see what you're saying, and I totally support give food to people in need. I'm just saying that I wouldn't be opposed to eating a sandwich a drinking a beer tonight. That's all."

"Fuck it, we'll get you the sandwich and the beer tonight," Arno said.

"Awesome," I said. "My second condition is that you have to make sure Johnny NEVER repeats these stories as his own. In fact, I really don't even want him to hear them."

"Fuck you," Johnny said.

"Done," Arno answered.

"What?" Johnny questioned.

"Listen, Johnny. I could cut the tension between you two with a knife. I have a feeling if you're down here listening you're going to be interrupting constantly. I won't be able to concentrate on the story itself," Arno continued. "Now, run across the street and grab a sandwich with the works on it for Beau, and pick up a six-pack of...what kind of beer do you like, Beau?"

"Something hoppy," I answered.

"Alright, grab a six pack of an IPA, Johnny," Arno said.

"But boss, don't we have someone else we can send do to this?"

"I asked you to do it, Johnny," Arno said sternly.

"Okay, no problem," Johnny said.

With a disgruntled look on his face, Johnny turned and slowly walked upstairs. He looked defeated. I almost felt sorry for him. Maybe I overreacted in excluding Johnny from the story. After all, he's just doing his mafia duties by roughing up a degenerate gambler. Should he have been a little more understanding due to our previous friendship? Sure, but I don't know why he's being such a Debbie downer. It's not like he's tied up in a chair with his impending death lingering over him. But that's neither here nor there. I needed to entertain a mafia boss. There was no time to worry about Johnny's feelings.

When Johnny had left the room, I began the story.

"Well, I guess the story really starts when my friend Mac told me about Key West, Florida. It was something he said that I had to confirm for myself.

"Dude...in Key West, you can literally be hammered drunk, butt naked, riding a unicycle while chugging a bottle of whiskey and yelling at cops without getting in any trouble. We HAVE to go!"

"I was sold. We went to Key West for Spring Break during our third year of college. Now, I'm able to confirm that Mac's statement was an absolute fact," I told Arno. "Spring break had always brought out my wild side, but this particular spring break took it to a new level. I suppose it had something to do with the white sand, crystal clear water, palm trees, perfect weather and girls surrounding me. Something about that combo just makes me get a little bit weird."

"I know exactly what you mean. I don't know how my wife can even blame me for having a gumar in those types of situation." Arno said.

"Gumar is your side girlfriend?"

"That's right. It's my favorite little tradition of ours," he answered.

"There are worse traditions out there," I continued, "Anyway, I was in Key West with a group of 10 friends. We were 21 and in fantastic partying shape. We could barely run a mile, but we could drink like fish. When we got to Key West - Mac, Chuck, Hallman and I quickly decided to engage in a case race. A case race is when every participant buys a case of beer. The rules are simple. The first one to finish their case wins. If you ever find yourself in a heated case race, here's some advice: don't sip on your beer. You'll lose. In order to speed up the process, we decided to buy a beer funnel. After this phenomenal purchase, we added a rule to the case race. There was to be no drinking from a can of beer. Every beer needed to be funneled. If you took a sip of beer, you were disqualified and left for dead."

"I might make my new guys do that sometime."

"You absolutely should. You never know what type of man someone is until you see him compete in a case race. That's what I always say at least. In fact, the mafia could probably avoid a lot of legal trouble if they initiated their members through case races instead of having them kill somebody."

"Get on with the story, smart guy," Arno ordered.

"Okay, here's the low down on the case race contenders. Mac could drink heavily, but whiskey with a splash of water is his normal choice. That meant he had a high tolerance, but his beer gut was smaller, which is a disadvantage in a case race. He's a taller guy, 6'2", tan, and has a full head of blonde hair. He was born and raised in Panama City, Florida. He started attending college Spring Breaks at age 13 and didn't miss one after. That's good experience for a case race."

"Alright, alright, who else?" Arno questioned impatiently.

"The person most likely to beat Mac in the case race would be Chuck. Chuck had been a close friend of Mac's from a young age. He was also born and raised in Panama City. Chuck was slightly shorter than Mac, but he had a much better beer gut. He attended the very same spring breaks as Mac, which meant most likely, at one point or another, the two had already competed against each other in a case race," I continued. "Next, there was Hallman. He was 5'10" and weighed about 180 lbs. He had tan skin and short dark brown hair. He was born and raised in Alabama. Hallman's best case-race attribute was that he was good at physically functioning after blacking out. That's a great attribute to have in these contests."

"Now, when you say, 'blackout', what exactly do you mean?" Arno asked.

"We drank to the point where we didn't remember drinking. It's waking up in a weird location and having absolutely no clue how you got there. It's not remembering peoples' names despite meeting them about 10 times."

"Why wouldn't you remember their names if you've met them 10 times?"

"Because I was already blackout when I met them. I've probably had 10 incredibly epic nights with them, but I don't remember it. The only people's names you remember are the ones you meet sober and/or the ones you spend the first three hours of the night with," I answered. "At some point in the night, you fall asleep in your head, and a robot version of you continues to party."

"That's not normal. Are you sure you're only drinking alcohol? Not mixing anything else?" Arno asked.

"Well, we also ate Xanax for breakfast in those days," I said.

"Xanax? The Anti-depressant?" He asked.

"That's the one," I confirmed.

"What in the hell did you college assholes spending your parents' money in exotic locations have to be depressed about?"

"Nothing." I said.

"Well, why did you eat anti-depressants for breakfast?"

"Because when you're not depressed, and then you take anti-depressants, all of a sudden you're in a pretty good mood. When you mix them with alcohol, despite the warning label warning against it, you tend to make bad decisions - but you have a hell of a time doing so."

"But, you didn't remember the night for yourself?" He asked.

"Well, some parts get a little hazy, that's for sure. Listen, I'm not trying to defend Xanax. I don't *ever* take them anymore. I'm pretty sure they're the reason why my memory is so terrible now. I'm just telling you what we did at the time. It was stupid, but it led to me being naked and painted in the streets of Key West. So, do you want to hear the rest of the story? Or would you like to criticize my past decision making a little more?" I asked.

"Careful, Beau. Careful. I've still got a pack of paper upstairs. College-ruled," Arno continued. "Now, continue the story."

"Okay. Finally there was me. I've always been a smaller guy, which has always led to me to trying to prove myself. I like being the underdog. I looked pretty much the same then as I do now." I was about 5'9, weighed 135 lbs., and I had dark hair with dark mustache to match. It was a bold lip sweater that gave me confidence. It was the first thing anyone ever noticed. It was so strong that nearly every person I encountered from age 18 and on commented on it. It was my pride and joy. This is the same mustache that you shaved by the way."

"Keep it up and I'll have one of those laser hair removal doctors come in here and do your upper lip," Arno said.

"I'm just pointing out facts," I continued. "Anyway, I probably wouldn't win the case-race, but while losing, I'd be chugging beer in the beautiful Florida Keys, with my mustache, so I'd still win."

"Naturally."

"The beers went down easy. Throughout the day, we became pro's. We each finished the first half of our cases within a couple hours. Those were light beers, so they went down like water. It took about 2 hours for us to down the next 10. Once we arrived at number 22, I decided to seize the day. Carpe diem. The race was a dead heat as we turned the last corner. I went for the victory. I went for the double funnel. I was going to chug two beers at once. However, Mac wasn't about to allow that. After 22 beers, you become less aware of your surroundings. Mac took advantage of this. While I was funneling my 23rd and 24th beer to finish my case,

Mac grabbed a plastic bottle of tequila, and squeezed it into the top of the funnel as I chugged."

"That bastard," Arno chimed in.

"Right?" I confirmed, "At first, I didn't think that even the cheapest tequila could slow me down on this particular night, and then my stomach realized it had been filled with cheap tequila. I spewed like a volcano. Vomit erupted through my mouth and nostrils. Vomiting through your nostrils is an experience that only alcoholics, or those on their way to being alcoholics, can appreciate, yet hate at the same time. Unfortunately, vomiting was an automatic disqualification from the case-race. Fortunately, I was too drunk to care. My thought process switched to finding a shower. After the shower, there would be food. There's nothing better than food when you're that drunk. The meal after that shower was the exact moment I started to like mustard."

"You didn't like mustard at one point?" Arno questioned in disbelief.

"Well, that's debatable. When I was younger, if I saw something that didn't look appealing to the eye, or didn't appeal to my sense of smell, I just went with the 'I don't like that food, and, of course I've tried it!' routine. So I suppose this was actually my first time eating mustard, and it was fantastic," I said.

"My son does the same thing. It drives me crazy," Arno admitted.

"Just get him really drunk and then take him out to eat," I advised.

"He's 14," Arno said.

"Okay, so maybe in another year or so?" I asked.

"Absolutely not. My son is going to Harvard. Not becoming a degenerate drunken gambler like yourself."

"Jesus, Arno. You might as well bust the paper back out if you're going to cut me that deep."

After a moment of silence, Arno gave a subtle, "Sorry, Beau. Now, please, continue."

"I don't even know if I feel like it now. I think I have to reflect on my entire life for an hour or so."

"Alright – if you're done I guess we'll just get the show on the road," Arno said as he pulled his pistol out and cocked it.

"Where was I?" I asked.

"You just got disqualified from the case-race and started to like mustard."

"Oh, yeah. Well - night rolled around. We were on Duvall Street, which is Key West's most popular downtown strip. The case race crew, along with three girls from school, Kimmy, Ashley and Molly, went to a bar called The Garden of Eden. It had three levels, but the rooftop level is the only one that matters for this story. The rooftop at the Garden of Eden is the only bar in Key West where clothing is optional. This bar has one rule, and one rule only: no sex on the premises. As soon as my friends and I walked in, we hit the bar."

"Just what you guys needed. More drinks," Arno said.

Before I could continue the story, the door opened and shut. Johnny trotted down the stairs.

"That was fast," Arno said.

Johnny handed the brown paper sandwich bag and a six-pack of beers to Arno. I wasn't sure if I'd ever drink another beer again. This was a game-changer.

Johnny turned and ran back up the stairs without saying a word.

"He's in a good mood," I said.

"He's been that way recently," Arno continued as he lit his cigar. "Now listen, Beau. I'm going to untie you so you can eat and drink. I swear to God, if you try ANYTHING, I will *fuck you up.* I'll put this cigar out in your eye. You got that?"

"I've never understood anything more clearly in my life," I answered.

Excitement boiled inside of me. I couldn't wait to stretch my arms. This was about to be glorious. They've been tied behind my back for quite a while. When the knots came loose, it felt so good that I went into a laughing attack.

"Not bad, eh?" Arno asked.

"Phenomenal," I said. I stretched my arms to the side. It was one of those stretches that made my whole body shake. I love those stretches. Next up: beer. I cracked the top and took a sip. Low and behold, another laughing attack.

"Hands down, the most I've ever appreciated a beer. No question," I said as I chuckled a bit more. I reached for the sandwich and unwrapped it. It had the works, mayo, lettuce, tomato, everything. Well done, Johnny. The first bite was so good that I almost wished Arno would've shot me in the face the moment I swallowed. It would've been going out on a high note.

"Let's get on with the story, Beau."

"Sounds good. Where were we?" I pondered. "Oh yeah, so as my friends and I were drinking at the bar, a topless lady approached us. Her boobs were painted in blue and purple psychedelic swirls, giving us an excuse to stare. After all, it wasn't our fault that they were painted with the sole purpose of being mesmerizing. She began to inform us about her body painting station. It was 100 dollars to have your body painted in detail. I thought it was way too expensive to be painted, so I completely zoned out of the conversation. I people watched. The body painter was tall. She was taller than I was. She was close to 6'0". She had chestnut brown hair, light skin and blue eyes. She was attractive. I would argue that she could have landed a better job elsewhere, instead of painting naked men and women at a bar in Key West, but I would lose that argument. Being able to live in Key West is worth having an absurd job."

"I've got to check this place out," Arno said.

"You need to get down there as soon as possible," I said. "When I snapped out of my daydream, I realized that everyone's eyes were on me."

"Do it, Beau!" Ashley cheered.

"Do what?" I asked her.

"Get painted!" She responded.

"Painted?"

"Painted," she said.

"I can't afford that."

"Did you not hear the conversation?" Ashley asked.

"Not a word of it."

"We're all going to chip in and pay for it!"

"Take your shorts off," the body painter demanded.

"I was in no condition to argue. I dropped my shorts to the ground," I said.

"Well..." I hesitated, "Let's do it, then."

"I took off my shirt and threw it to Molly. Now, I was fucking naked. If you ever find yourself in a situation like this, I cannot stress how important it is to keep a quarter-chub," I told Arno.

"A quarter-chub?" Arno questioned.

"A quarter chub," I answered. " It's when a man's penis is only slightly erected and gives the appearance of a massive soft penis. It's difficult to keep a quarter-chub for very long. More often that not, you're on your way to having an erection. However, if you can pull this off for an extended period of time, you can gain some serious street cred in a nude bar. The key to pulling this off is being just drunk enough to keep it at half-mask. I had successfully pulled this off and was feeling confident. I followed the lady to her painting stand and my friends followed behind me. I noticed Molly staring at me like I had stared at the artists' swirls. That couldn't be a bad thing."

"Can I call you swirls?" I asked.

"Call me whatever you want," Swirls continued. "I'm going to paint you into an octopus."

"Next lesson," I continued. "A fine tip paintbrush is a good thing. I didn't know how this octopus was going to be painted until Swirls pulled out her blue paint, that fine tip paintbrush, and proceeded to trace the octopus body over my stomach. The top of the octopus's body began at my sternum, and the bottom ended at my waistline – it was the exact same pattern you cut me. She then went to my thighs, and painted tentacles hanging down. There were three tentacles on my left thigh and four on my right. After that, my penis was painted as the eighth tentacle. I was the dicktopus.

"Ridiculous," Arno chimed in.

"I mingled throughout the bar, where it didn't take long to notice a trend. I was receiving free drinks from a lot older women. Grandmas have always loved me and it's easy to flirt with them if you're bold enough to try. When I say older women, I'm talking about silver fox women. Not your standard 40 to 55 year old extremely attractive woman who still has her natural hair color. Not the doctor's wife who has been rebuilt to an awkward perfection. I'm talking about a woman with wrinkles. I'm talking about a woman with a full head of silver hair. They were their in numbers – most of them with their husbands. The husbands were fine with me taking pictures with their wives. They just wanted to see a 21 year-old female walking around naked. At the end of the night, I had the ability to say I've taken shots with more 60 year-old married couples while in the nude than most people in the entire world can say. I'd say I'm in the top thousand in that category."

"Your mother must be so proud," Arno said.

"Debatable," I continued. "After a while, I noticed that my friends had gathered my clothes, which was a relief. I was not in the 'keep up with my clothes' mindset. I turned around with the grin that had become frozen on my face and saw Molly walking towards me like she was on a mission. Molly was sexy. She had long blonde hair, green eyes and was dressed promiscuously. When she had made her way through the crowd and face-to-face with me, she firmly gripped my eighth tentacle," I said.

"Let's go," Molly said.

"I was helpless. We stumbled into the bathroom stall. We were going to break the only rule this bar had. I stood next to the toilet and she dropped to her knees. It was sanitary. Visions of an octopus with a human head raced through my mind. Within moments, the bathroom stall swung open and the bouncer stood over us," I told Arno.

"Uh oh!" Arno said excitedly.

It reminded me of how excited kids get during a ghost story. I don't know why story time stops all of a sudden once you get to a certain age. People expect you to read the stories yourself. It's not as much fun. Adults need story-time too. Even mafia bosses do.

"Let's go," a grisly man who was at least three times my size told me.

"The first 'let's go' was much better," I responded.

"Our friends noticed Molly and I being dragged out. I was sent airborne into the middle of Duvall Street. I stood up and looked at Molly. Her face was smeared with blue. My quarter-chub returned. However, the sound of a familiar voice canceled out any joy the sight of Molly's blue face gave me.

"Beau?"

"Who was it?" Arno asked.

"My worst nightmare. It was a group of 20 girls." I said.

"20 girls?" Arno asked, "What in the hell could be so bad about that?"

"Normally, this would not be a bad thing. On this particular occasion, it was a bad thing. It was my ex-girlfriend, Afton. We had dated for almost 2 years and had ended our relationship about six months before that. She was accompanied by 19 of her closest sorority sisters," I informed him.

"Oh, well...fuck," Arno said.

"That's right, Arno. Fuck."

"What was that about? WHOA! Are you painted?"

"They had noticed the octopus. Next, they noticed Molly's blue face. My tentacle was on display for the world to see. The next thing I know, Afton's open right palm landed with a thud across my face. It was the hardest slap I've ever received. Hands down."

"You mean to tell me that a college girl slapped you harder than I did the other day?" Arno asked in disbelief.

"No contest. I had honestly totally forgotten that you slapped me. I tell stories of this girl's slap. It was legendary."

"You forgot!" Arno said.

"It's not your fault," I said in an attempt to console him. "Afton had a deep hatred for me burning in her heart at the time and she let it all come out with one slap. She swung as hard as she could. It was probably her first slap. How many slaps have you dished out?" I asked.

"Thousands," Arno said.

"Well, there you have it," I continued. "The slap you gave me the other day was just another day at the office for you. For Afton, it was a chance to slam a bad chapter of her life shut, and she slammed it shut. You basically put a bookmark in and gently put the book on the bookshelf," I said.

"I guess that makes sense," he said.

"Have you ever been slapped really hard, Arno?"

"Nobody, and I mean NOBODY, would ever be that stupid. They'd lose their hands," Arno said in a stern tone.

"Because of a slap? Nobody likes an over-reaction. You could be legendary if you were cool as a cucumber in situations where being intense wasn't necessary. Then everyone would love you and fear you."

"I'll tell you this once, Beau. Don't give me advice on being the boss. It upsets me."

"Noted," I said. Despite Arno getting slightly upset at my suggestion, I could tell that he was thinking about it afterwards. His mind was wandering. "I watched Afton walk away, took a deep breath, slid my shirt over my head, turned in the opposite direction and there she was, no more than 10 feet in front of me."

"There who was?" Arno asked from the edge of his seat.

"It was a naked woman, riding a unicycle, chugging a bottle of whiskey. Her entire body was painted and she was yelling at police officers. The police officers simply stared, supporting quarter-chubs of their very own as she rode away into the night."

"Fuck you," Arno replied.

"It's a true story," I confirmed.

"You're not embarrassed about that night at all?"

"I guess I hit a few low points throughout the night, but overall, it was just what I needed."

"You *needed* to be painted like an octopus?"

"Well, no, I didn't necessarily need to be painted like an octopus, but I had been doing the exact same thing every single day before that spring break. I needed to wake up. It snapped me out of the funk I was in, for a little while, at least. I went back to school with twice as much confidence in myself as I had before." I said.

"I know just what you mean, and I'm sold. I'm booking a flight to Key West. I'll be back in a couple of days. Johnny will be in charge," Arno said.

"What? Are you serious?"

"Dead serious," he answered. "I need to wake up, too. I've been thinking too much recently."

The door swung open and Johnny trotted back down.

"Hey boss man," Johnny started.

"Johnny, I'm going to Key West for a couple of days," Arno interrupted. "You're in charge."

Johnny looked at me and smiled.

"Beau better be in the same condition he's in now when I get back," Arno said.

I returned Johnny's smile with one of my own.

"Now, Beau, chug that beer so we can get out of here."

I did as he said. It was delightful. When I was finished, I crushed the can and handed it to him.

"See you soon," Arno said as he stood up.

Arno stood up and gave me a few pats on my bare back right shoulder. For some reason, it hurt, enough for me to give a slight gasp.

"I don't remember fucking your shoulder up, Beau."

"It's probably from when I 'fell' to the ground - when I got to Johnny's Grandmas'," I said.

"I'll take a quick look," he said.

Arno stood up and took a glance.

"Looks like a bruise," he said. "Wait, is that a tattoo, Beau?" he asked.

"It's probably both," I answered.

Arno leaned closer so he could examine the tattoo.

"Fuck Milkshakes?"

"It's a long story," I said.

My lone tattoo was on my back right shoulder. It was not the first time someone had been confused by it, but it made sense to me. The tattoo was an image of a large vanilla milkshake with whipped cream and a cherry on top. This milkshake was inside a large red circle with the diagonal slash through it, or the universal "no" symbol. The words "Fuck Milkshakes" were written in cursive directly below the image.

"What's it about?" Arno asked.

"A wired-shut jaw."

"When I get back from Key West, I want to hear it. That is, if you're available and all."

"I'll need to check my schedule, but I should be free. Now, what do you think about potentially tying my arms up in a different position this time around? I mean, if you could tie them up while they're resting on the arm rests, that would be incredible," I suggested.

"Fuck it, I'm feeling generous. But, let me reiterate, if you try anything, I will fuck you up," Arno informed.

"Noted," I answered. "What are your thoughts on me pulling the reclining lever?" I asked.

"Go for it," Arno said.

I reclined, and moved my arms to the armrest. Being tied up didn't even seem like a big deal with this new setup. Arno and Johnny hit the lights off and left. I fell asleep with a smile on my face. It was a good day in captivity indeed.

Chapter X

WINNIE

Meanwhile, in North Carolina...

"911, what's your emergency?" An operator answered.

"I need to report a missing person," Winnie said in her 1920s, Southern Alabama accent. It's a lovely accent to listen to. It doesn't make her sound uneducated. She speaks slowly, but properly. She drags the end of her words out into her own little twist, giving her a beautifully unique voice. Winnie married my Grandpa, Wally, and moved to North Carolina right after they both graduated from Auburn University. Sadly, after fifty years of marriage, Wally died. Now, Winnie sits at the top of the family tree.

"When was the last time you were in contact with this person?"

"It's been a week and a day since I've heard from him. We've spoken on the phone every single Tuesday for 10 years. Yesterday was the first Tuesday he hasn't called me. I'm just worried sick!"

"What is the missing person's name?"

"Beau Allen."

"Date of Birth?"

"September 3, 1987. He's 27."

"Birth place?"

"Winston-Salem, North Carolina," Winnie answered.

"Does Beau have any nicknames he goes by?" The operator questioned.

"Not that I know of. He lives in Brooklyn, New York, now."

"And what is your relation to Beau?"

"He's my Grandson, that poor baby."

"And your name is?"

"Paula Allen, but everyone calls me Winnie," Winnie delivered eloquently. It was a line that she had been saying for years.

"Okay. Now, Winnie, do you know of anyone else that Beau normally contacts? Any family or friends?" The operator questioned.

"I've called his parents. Nobody has heard from him," Winnie said.

"Can you give me a physical description of Beau?"

"He's about 5'9", slim, brown hair brushed to the side, brown eyes, and he has a thick mustache." Winnie answered.

"Does he have any tattoos?" The operator questioned.

"Just one. It's a milkshake on his back right shoulder. I completely disapproved of it," Winnie said.

"Do you know if Beau drinks, smokes, or uses any recreational drugs?"

"Well, Beau is no perfect angel, but he's a sweet as can be!" Winnie replied.

"Is Beau currently employed?" The operator asked.

"Two Tuesdays ago he was searching for a job. I've been expecting to hear that he got a job over that time period. Instead I'm filling out a police report."

"Do you have his current address in Brooklyn? We'll relay the information to the Brooklyn Police Department."

"Yes, I've got it right here. It's 4200 Hancock St., Brooklyn, NY 11237," Winnie answered.

"And your phone number please? We'll have the Brooklyn PD contact you after they look over this information."

"555-786-6771," Winnie replied.

"Okay, great. Now, Winnie, what I would suggest from here would be to call all of Beau's relatives and friends, ask them if they've seen Beau, and if not, make them aware that Beau may be missing. Also, it would be a good idea to post some flyers around the Brooklyn area."

"I'll make some calls right this very moment and then book a flight to New York," Winnie informed.

"Great. Stay by the phone today, Winnie. I'm sure the Brooklyn Police Department will contact you shortly," The operator said.

"I'll have it right by my side. Thanks for your help, you've been just wonderful, sweetheart," Winnie remarked.

"It's no problem at all, and we will do everything in our power to bring Beau home to you safe and sound," the operator continued. "We'll be in touch soon."

"Perfect, bye now," Winnie closed.

She hung up the phone and booked her flight. Winnie was now on the case.

Chapter XI

JOHNNY

The next day was a bad one. I dreamt about Key West for the few hours that I was able to sleep and thought about it while I was awake. Dreaming about the keys would normally be a good thing. For me, it was terrible, because when I snap out of the daydream, I'm still tied to a chair. There was way too big of a drop off.

On a bright note, my two sandwich deliveries had a little variety to them. The first one was turkey and cheese. The second delivery was roast beef and cheese. Both sandwiches had the works. It was glorious. I was starting to think Arno might like me enough to let me off the hook. I even felt kind of "full" after eating the second sandwich. If I could get the remainder of that six pack, I'd have no complaints.

I heard the door open and close. It was the first time they had not slammed it shut, and it almost scared me more. Obviously, someone is eventually going to come downstairs. There wasn't that much to be nervous about at this point. It's kind of like the waiting room in a Dentist office. I know for a fact that one of the assistants is going to come and call my name, but it's still hard to prepare for. As soon as the assistant does call my name, I hate it.

The basement door opened and the lights flicked on. It was Johnny and a man wearing doctor's scrubs with a white lab coat. If you think seeing a doctor at his practice is nerve-racking, then you should try seeing one down here. When Johnny got in front of me, I noticed that he was carrying a plastic bucket.

"What's in the bucket Johnny?" I asked.

Before a reply could come, I knew what was in the bucket. It was ice-cold water. *SPLASH!*

I screamed and then carried it into laughter.

"Morning, Beau," Johnny said casually.

"I was awake before the ice water, you dick."

"Were you? I didn't notice," Johnny continued. "Beau, meet Dr. Stone."

"What's shakin' doc?"

Dr. Stone was a shorter guy, about 5'6", with black hair and glasses. Without replying, Dr. Stone sat down and got to work.

"Don't ask him any questions," Johnny interrupted. "Now, did you have fun with Arno yesterday?"

"Is that what this is about? Also, is it nighttime right now? How long has it been since Arno was here?"

"I'm not going to tell you," Johnny said.

"Doc, is it nighttime?" I asked. He looked at me with a blank stare.

"Don't tell him, Doc," Johnny said.

"Okay. I'm just going to assume it's nighttime, and I promise I'll try to keep track from now on."

"Shut the fuck up, Beau. Doc, get to work."

"Chill, Johnny, I can tell you the story if you want to hear it that badly," I said.

"I don't give a fuck about the story. What I give a fuck about is Arno being in Key West because of you."

"Why would you care about that?"

"Frankly, because some of us work very hard for Arno and would have appreciated an invite," Johnny admitted.

"You're not the jealous type, are you, Johnny?"

"Fuck you, Beau."

"I think he went on a find-himself type of journey, anyways."

"He's the boss of the family, not a hippie. Stop filling his head with nonsense," Johnny snapped.

"Hippies aren't the only ones who can go on a journey to broaden their horizons."

"See what I mean, doc? This is going to be necessary in order to shut him the fuck up."

"What's going to be necessary?" I asked.

"You'll see," Johnny replied. "Now, doc, how long is this thing going to take? I've got somewhere I've got to be."

"Not long," Dr. Stone muttered.

Dr. Stone seemed to be scared.

"Are you in debt to this asshole, too?" I asked him.

"Shut the fuck up, Beau," Johnny said.

The look in Dr. Stone's eyes gave it away though. He was definitely being forced to do this.

"Do it, Doc," Johnny said as he returned my recliner to its upright position.

"Wait a second here," I continued, "Arno said I wouldn't be fucked with while he was away."

"Oh yeah? Well, I'll tell him I did a 'finding myself' journey too, and part of finding out who I really am involved wiring your jaw shut," Johnny replied.

"Wait, what?" I asked.

"Chill, Beau. We're not about to kill you. We're not even going to hurt you. You'll be perfectly fine - you'll just unable to speak for a while."

"I hate you," I said as I tried to use brute force to burst out of the ropes. It didn't work.

"You're reminding me how great of an idea it is to do this," Johnny responded.

Dr. Stone grabbed a chair, slid it next to the small table on my left, and sat down. He pulled out his tools, and set them on the table.

"Sorry about that, Doc," Johnny continued. "You're going to want to bust out the anesthetic. Beau, consider that a slight apology from me for being an asshole. I've heard your broken jaw story. I know how much you enjoy these shots. You're lucky that I'm not actually going to break your jaw before having it wired shut."

"I'd prefer an apology by not wiring my jaw shut."

"Too bad."

The doctor tapped the needle and wiped my arm with an alcohol pad.

"I'm sorry for spitting in your face, Doc."

"That's alright," he responded.

I wonder how much cash he owes Johnny? I'd bet it's more than me. He is a doctor after all. He has a lot more money to play around with. If I were a Doctor I probably would have lost a million on that last cold streak. Dr. Stone injected the needle into my arm. I had been under anesthesia a few times before. It's not too shabby. The split second before I pass out is a feeling of complete euphoria.

"Johnny - we're going to need your grandma, pot roast, and a blender," I mumbled into unconsciousness.

CHAPTER XII

FUCK MILKSHAKES - PART ONE

It was pitch black when I woke up. It had that "waking up in the middle of the night" feeling to it, in the neighborhood of 3 a.m. It took a moment to remember what had happened - only a moment, though. After that, I experienced a terrible feeling. It was one that I had felt before. I tried to yawn with a wired-shut jaw.

Yawning was no longer an option. I was angry. For the second time, I tried to parlay my anger into brute strength and bust out of the chair. This time, I felt like I created a little wiggle room on my right wrist rope. However, after flexing for a good minute and half, I felt exhausted. The exhaustion threw me into my next stage, the crying stage. I cried, and I cried hard. My morale was at an all-time low.

My mind raced and raced with terrible thoughts. It was the first time I truly hated somebody. Well, I'm not sure if that's entirely true. It depends what the line between a strong dislike and hate is. I strongly dislike lima beans, country music, not having a mustache, the sound of a baby crying, and people who are assholes in restaurants, especially if that asshole has a crying baby with them.

I dislike Johnny more than all of that stuff.

BAM!

The upstairs door opened and slammed. It probably happened at the perfect time, too. My thoughts were getting pretty morbid for a second there. The basement door opened and the lights flicked on. It was Arno, and despite the fact that this man would probably be responsible for my death, I was glad he was back.

"Beau-diddly!"

Arno seemed to be in a good mood. However, I was not. I did not respond. I simply showed all of my teeth.

"That's a mighty big smile you have going on there, Beau. I didn't think you'd be *that* happy to see me!"

"I'm not fucking smiling," I said.

"Well...what are you doing then?"

"Come have a look at my mouth."

Arno moved in closer and squinted to focus.

"Did you have braces when I left for Key West?"

"They're not braces."

"They look like braces to me."

"Look closer."

Arno moved in even closer and saw the difference between braces and what I had.

"Whoa. Are you fucking locked in there?" He asked.

"That's one way to put it. My jaw is wired shut."

"Who did this? What happened?"

I came close to going on a rant about how much I fucking hate Johnny, but then a very important thought came to mind. Mobsters hate snitches.

"Doesn't matter," I said. "Can we just un-wire it, please?"

"Eventually, sure. Let's wait a bit, though. I did say we were going to knock everything off your worst nightmares list. You said you'd rather die than have your jaw wired shut again. I was going to give you that option. I was going to have a doctor either break your jaw and wire it shut, or if you so chose, I was going to shoot you. After getting to know you a bit, I feel like you would've been an asshole and asked for the bullet."

His response made me a bit sick to my stomach. I thought we had already become close enough to avoid the rest of that torture/death ordeal. Apparently he had not forgotten.

"You're probably right. In retrospect, I definitely over-reacted by saying I'd rather be dead. A wired-shut jaw is incredibly annoying, but it's tolerable," I said.

"Well you're in luck, Beau. I know an oral surgeon who owes me a favor. I'll get him to get those wires off as soon as possible."

"That is excellent news."

"Don't mention it."

"How was Key West?"

"What can I say? It was great. You were right. I had an adrenaline rush. It woke me up. It was exactly what I needed. I tried to ride a unicycle, butt naked, chugging a bottle of tequila while yelling at the cops."

"You what?"

"I'm kidding, kind of. Long story short, I had an adrenaline rush by running from the cops. I guess the they're more prejudiced towards naked old men than they are towards naked young women."

"What happened?" I asked.

"The unicycle happened. I tried to ride it, but I crashed."

"Was it a bad crash?"

"I flipped over the hood of a parked cop car."

"What'd they do?"

"They tried to arrest me."

"Tried?"

"Beau, one thing you might not know about me is, despite being old, I can run from cops like a cheetah."

"You got away from the cops? Naked? On foot?"

"That's right."

"No way, how the did you manage to do that?"

"Well, I got up faster than the cops and dipped into the closest alley way I could find. From there, I ran a couple blocks and then made another turn, but when I sprinted around the corner, I collided with one of the cops who was chasing after me. We collided so hard that it knocked him out cold. From there, I just ran towards the sound of water and jumped into the ocean. When the coast was clear, I stole a beach towel and headed back to Garden of Eden to grab my clothes and wallet. After getting dressed, I just casually walked out of there and went back to the hotel."

"God, I love Key West."

"Me too, Beau...me, too."

"Are you going to go back?"

"Absolutely."

"I probably won't get a chance to," I said in an attempt to make Arno feel sorry for me.

"You know, you speak pretty good with a wired-shut jaw," Arno said, ignoring my previous statement.

"I know I do. I've had a good bit of practice before today."

"That's right! The "Fuck Milkshakes" tattoo! You were going to tell me about the first wired-shut jaw!"

"You want to hear it right now?" I asked.

"I couldn't think of a more perfect time, Beau. I mean, how often do you get to tell a story about your previously wired-shut jaw, with your jaw currently wired shut?"

"Hopefully not too often."

"It's perfect! We have to do it now."

"Are you going to get the doctor back tomorrow to unwire this shit?"

"Consider it done, Beau. Consider it done."

"Well, let me start at the end. I got this tattoo as a celebration. My jaw had finally been unwired."

"How long was it wired for?"

"14 weeks."

"14 weeks without real food. I can't even imagine."

"My jaw was shattered. My jaw broke right by my right ear and my chin was basically knocked off."

"Ouch," Arno said.

"It was miserable. I just sat in my parent's house, 21 years old, wasting my prime with a shattered jaw held together by wires. Every day, when I got hungry, I'd go to the freezer and grab one of the containers of frozen pot roast that my mom had made in bulk for me. I'd thaw it out and add half-and-half so that it would blend into liquid. After that, I'd drink through my stainless steel straw."

"Stainless steel straw?" Arno questioned.

"That's right. A stainless steel straw may be the single most important item I owned when my jaw was wired shut. It kept me from seeing my blended food, which tends to look disgusting," I continued. "Once I had my blended pot roast ready, I fought like a Spartan to get the blended pot roast to work its way up my straw and give me a brief remembrance of the taste of food. It often resulted in the sound of slurping, which I felt bad about."

"I hate the sound of slurping," Arno said.

"As you should," I continued. "Unfortunately, in this situation, there wasn't anything that I could do about it."

"Now I'm definitely getting the doctor in here to take those wires off. Constant slurping might convince me to shoot you."

"I wouldn't blame you. I'd shoot me, too."

Arno pulled out his cell phone and dialed a number. He didn't seem to be in a patient mood. After a few moments, he said, "Dammit, no answer."

"Like I was saying, sitting in my parent's house was a result of the worst bet I've ever made. Well, up until now, that is. There was only one positive from the experience. My grades were due to come out about a week later. They were going to be terrible. However, by the time they came out, my parents were sympathetic towards me because my jaw was shattered. That was clutch."

"You're lucky you have such forgiving parents. If you were my son I would've punched you in your wired-shut jaw for being such a moron. I don't tolerate bad grades."

"Well, this is a rock bottom story. I eventually figured out the whole 'college' thing and graduated," I continued. "But my parents were bewildered by my terrible grades at the time. Every reason I told them for my lack of production was bullshit. The extreme partying was the reason. I had a simple logic for feeding my parents lie after lie, and that was so I could stay in college, enjoying the high-life, pun intended. The goal was to not have to go home and feel like a complete loser. It had almost become a game I played with my parents, how creative could I become in the lying department on the spur of the moment when my parents would call? I like to think that George Costanza would have been proud. In fact, I still haven't told my parents what *really* happened on the night that left my jaw shattered. I told them I got blindside punched, and that I don't have the slightest idea who threw the punch."

"Your parents still don't know what happened?"

"Of course not!" I said. "They'd probably make me pay them back for the jaw surgeries."

"I'd make you pay me back triple the amount," Arno said. "What *actually* happened?

I got confident, and decided to make a bet. Behind the confidence to make this bet was the last Xanax I ever ate. After the Xanax bar there were a few beers, a couple of larger than average vodka tonics with splashes of lime, one shot of cheap tequila and the casual puff or two of marijuana, naturally."

"Of course," Arno chimed in.

"At the peak of this decision was the bet itself, which was to decide whether or not my buddy, Hallman, could knock me out cold with one swing of his fist. I had, we'll I didn't have, but I bet $500 that he could not do it."

"You bet someone $500 bucks that they couldn't knock you out cold with a free punch?"

"Yes, I did."

"You're a fucking moron." Arno informed me.

"I know, but I liked my odds. Up to that point, it was a known fact that I had an iron jaw. I had been punched in the face about 100 times and I had never fallen to the ground. I felt invincible. I knew with certainty that Hallman did not have $500 either, but my attitude at this point in life was still 'fuck it, why not?' I was on the verge of flunking out of college. Instead of actually giving a shit, I raged on a nightly basis. I figured I'd enjoy the end of my days there. As odd as it sounds, when you're at rock bottom, being punched in the face, hard, can be enjoyable. It's another one of those things that can get you jump-started. Feeling down? Ask someone to punch me in the face - or go skydiving."

Arno quickly stood up, and punched me in the right eye.

"What the hell!" I yelled in pain.

"That 'fuck it' attitude sounds like the one that landed you in this basement."

"It is pretty similar, isn't it?" I continued as I blinked my watering eye. "At least I don't eat Xanax now."

"It's all about the small victories for you, isn't it, Beau?"

"Better than focusing on the massive losses," I replied.

"Touché."

Chapter XXIII

FUCK MILKSHAKES - PART TWO

"I love summertime!" I shouted to Hallman. "It's so much better than the rest of the year."

"Me too, man!" Hallman shouted back. "Only an hour away from drink specials."

"I hear you, dude," I responded

"You want to split another Xanax before downtown?" Hallman questioned.

"I thought about it briefly. I knew that I would be out of control if I said 'yes.'

"Yes," I said.

"Wednesday night was always the best night of the week, due to Sky Bar's drink specials from 7 to 9. These specials included 32 oz. mixed liquor drinks for three dollars - a dangerous combination for someone with fifty dollars to their name. We had one hour to build up what I considered to be the necessary amount of liquid confidence to properly enjoy drinking these monstrous liquor drinks."

Arno shook his head.

"Forty-five minutes later we were robotically walking the four blocks from my apartment to the bar. As we were walking, we stopped in front of Crabbie's Seafood and stared at the lobster tank through the window.

"Think how miserable it would be to be a lobster in one of those tanks at a seafood restaurant," I continued. "I mean, do you think they've figured out what's going on?"

"I don't know, man. They're fucking lobsters," Hallman responded.

"I realize that, but surely not all of them get cooked on a daily basis. Some of those lobsters have witnessed a big net scoop their friends up, or arms grabbing them from above. What I'm asking is - do you think there is one lobster in the Crabbie's tank that has somehow avoided the chef's selection for a few days and realized that all of his bro's were being eaten at the tables surrounding him every single night?"

"I'd say yes," Hallman answered.

"I think so, too. Why do you think they know what's going on?" I questioned.

"Because they look suspicious."

"Lobsters look suspicious?"

"I think so. They're aliens in my opinion."

"Aliens?"

"Aliens. They live in a crazy environment, and they look like what I imagine aliens to look like. Not just lobsters, though. Pretty much everything that lives at the bottom of the deep ocean is an alien," Hallman ranted. "Plus, suspicious people normally know what's going on. I don't see why that would be any different for suspicious lobsters."

"So you think the Lobsters in the tanks at Crabbie's know they're about to be someone's dinner?" I asked.

"I think they do," Hallman answered. "In a seafood restaurant's lobster tank, it's all about the survival of the un-fittest. You need to make yourself look as unpresentable as possible."

"Good call," I continued. "If I'm a lobster at Crabbie's, I'm starting a hunger strike and ignoring the flakes of food they dump in the tank.

"Do you think that the restaurant feeds the lobsters or do they just assume they'll cook them fast enough to not have to feed them?" Hallman asked.

"If I were a betting man, well, I am a betting man, so I'd put my money on they get fed," I said.

"Speaking of that, does someone make flakes of food for lobsters like they do for goldfish?" Hallman asked.

"Absolutely, why wouldn't they?" I continued. "With all the seafood restaurants in America that have the tanks with lobsters, I think it would be a decent-sized business."

"You may have a point. If there's not already a monopoly on the lobster food business, we should look into starting one up," he said, beginning to slur a bit.

"Absolutely," I continued. "Let's roll."

"You two were smart. I'm shocked you had problems in school," Arno said.

"I was too, Arno. I was too," I began. "We arrived at Sky Bar just as drink specials began. Our goal was to drink at least three 32 oz. vodka-tonics before the two hours were over. If I could knock back at least three of these drinks, I would be wasted for less than ten dollars. I saw that as a huge success."

"Who wouldn't?" Arno joked.

"Anyway, as the night continued and Hallman and I increased our blood alcohol level, we began to argue over any and every topic, simply for the sake of arguing. It was something we always seemed to do. The goal was always to humorously talk trash to one another. You needed to sting your opponent deep with your words, but at the same time, make them laugh," I said.

"My guys and I are busting balls all the time," Arno admitted.

"After a few more failed attempts at one-night stands with random girls, we ran into a few of our buddies. Will, Hamp and Field. They were frat guy/hippie hybrids. They were best friends, and at the bar five nights a week.

"What's up amigos?" I greeted.

"Not much, man. We're about to cruise to my house for a night cap," Will continued. "We're going to load up the bong and try to finish the keg from earlier if y'all are interested?"

"Interested?" Hallman continued. "Abso-fucking-lutely!"

"The five of us left Sky Bar and headed for Will's house, leaving three out of our five debit cards behind in the process. It seemed like we got there in a flash. We filled our beer glasses to the brim. Soon after that, the bong was loaded. We sat around Will's 'smoking' station, a small circle formed using leather ottomans. In the center of the ottomans there was a coffee table that opened up. The bong and weed were hidden inside. It didn't take long before the room was hazy. My body was numb and my speech was slurred, but the party went on. When we went outside to burn a cigarette, the really bad decisions started flowing."

"Alright!" Arno exclaimed.

"A popular drunk topic of conversation among boys arrived once our cigarette were lit. We reminisced about previous fights we had been in. What a *stupid* fucking topic, but since it arose so frequently, our verbal jabs towards each other were on point."

"*I've never been knocked down by a punch - ever!*" I bragged

"*Ever?*" Field Questioned.

"*Fucking ever, Field,*" I responded.

"*He's full of shit,*" Hallman continued. "*A light breeze could knock him over.*"

"*Fuck you, Hallman - you've seen me get rocked in the face at least five times.*"

"*Yeah, but they were all weaklings. I could knock you out, no questions asked,*" Hallman said as he high-fived Will.

"*Challenge!*" Hamp chimed in.

"*I'll second that emotion,*" Will said.

"*Well...why stop there?*" I questioned. "*Let's make it interesting.*"

"*Do you really want to pay me to knock you out?*"

"*Name your price,*" I said.

"*$100 bones,*" Hallman challenged.

"*You're not very confident in this, are you?*"

"*$200 bones,*" he responded.

"*$500 bones,*" I said.

"*$500?*" Hallman asked.

"*$500.*"

"*I don't have $500 to bet,*" he said.

"Neither do I. We'll settle up one day," I said.

"Done," he said.

"Fuck yeah!" said Will.

"I've got the camera ready!" Hamp exclaimed.

"The five of us walked out onto the front porch of the house. It was almost show time. The camera started rolling. Despite the vast amount of drugs, alcohol, and weed coursing through my body, I still felt nervous. Butterflies were fluttering viciously in my stomach."

"First," I announced. "Some ground rules. The bet is that Hallman cannot knock me to the ground with one punch."

"Hear, hear!" The group cheered.

"Second, Hallman, you're not allowed to crow hop into the punch."

"Come on, now. Do you honestly think I'm going to need a crow hop?" Hallman said with a laugh of disbelief.

"Lastly, I get to grab Will and Field's shoulder for a bit of support."

"No problem. Will, Field, I'm sorry if I hit him so hard that y'all hit the ground, too." Hallman said.

"You're just pissing me off, Hallman. It's psyching me up."

"Not even Vince Lombardi could psyche you up enough to withstand this punch."

"Alright, well...fuck it then," I said.

"Hallman stepped back and took a few practice swings. I remember my gut telling me that it was a bad idea. He was swinging with some thunder. Will and

Field leaned over. My right hand gripped into Will's shirt and my left into Field's. I dug my feet in to the sidewalk the best that I was able to for balance. I leaned my head forward - essentially teeing up my chin for Hallman's driver.

BAM!

"The sound of a slow wind lingered throughout my head. The slow wind morphed into the sound of voices."

"OHHHHHHHHH!" The group cheered.

"When my sight faded back in, I found myself still standing."

"You didn't go down?" Arno asked.

"I didn't go down. I heard a loud noise, but I didn't feel a thing. When I shook my head I felt blood begin to flow over my bottom lip and onto the ground below."

"I'm up," I said in a daze.

"Will, Hamp, Field and Hallman's jaws were all dropped wide open."

"500 bones," I said as I spat more blood out.

"I still wasn't able to feel a thing at this point. My face felt like it had been stuck with 20 shots of Novocain."

"Here's your tooth, dude," Hamp told me as he handed me what looked like a shark tooth.

"Which one?" I questioned while opening my mouth

"Holy shit, man," Will continued. "You need to get to the hospital. It's one of the middle teeth on the bottom. It's gushing blood."

"I can't believe how big my tooth is," I said as I stared at the bloodied tooth.

"Clench your teeth together," Will said.

"When I did this, I knew I was fucked. The top molars on the right side of my mouth came down completely outside of my lower molars."

"Dude, your jaw is fucked up!" Will exclaimed.

"Yeah," Hamp continued. "That calls for an immediate trip to the Emergency Room."

"Fuck!" I said. "My parents are going to kill me!"

"I'll drive," Hallman said.

"I don't think that's a good idea at all!" Will insisted.

"The last five minutes sobered me up," Hallman continued. "I'm good."

"I'll call a taxi," Will said.

"Well - y'all want to do a quick smoke session before you roll?" Field joked.

"Absolutely," I answered.

"Seriously?" Field laughed, "I was joking dude."

"I wasn't," I continued. "One more bong for good luck. They're not going to give me any pain pills while I'm this drunk."

"Well," Field continued after glancing at Will and Hamp. "Might as well."

"Back to the smoking station we went," I said.

"You fucking morons," Arno said. It was another one of those classic Arno lines that I ignore.

"Will threw me some paper towels and I held them against my mouth. My hand was completely covered in blood. Field loaded the bong and passed it over to me."

"Here you go, dude, enjoy," Field said.

"I grasped the bong with my left hand and the lighter with my right. I ripped it until I filled the bong with a thick smoke. I pulled the slide and breathed in deep like it was the last breath I'd ever take. What came next was that moment when you've realized that you've taken too big of a hit. There's a split second where only *you* know it. That moment always ends quickly, and when it does, the rest of the group knows you bit off more than you could chew. In this particular instance, my result was a violent cough! I couldn't control it. I coughed six or seven times and then attempted to take a quick, deep breath. However, I took too deep of a breath. It led me to one last *extremely* harsh cough. Some drool/blood mixture dropped from my bottom lip! My eyes filled with so much water I lost my vision. After drying my eyes, I saw what I had done."

"Oh, shit!" I continued. "My bad, dude."

"Hallman, Hamp and Field were all laughing uncontrollably. Will, who so graciously allowed these tomfooleries to take place in his house, was now *covered* in my blood, and so was his bong."

"Sorry, Will," I continued. "On that note, Hallman, you ready to do this?" I questioned.

"Let's roll," Hallman responded.

"The blood covering my right hand has dried. I clinched my fist and extended it towards Will, Hamp and Field."

"Bloody pound it," I said.

"Hamp and Bo accepted the sign of 'all is well.' They gave the bloody fist bump. Will just stared. I turned to walk out of the house. As I got to the door, Will spoke up."

"Just remember, this did not happen at my house," Will said.

"That's a given, dude. That's a given," I responded.

"Will then walked over and pounded my bloody fist. Hallman and I walked outside. The cab was waiting. I hoped in the passenger seat. It seemed like I just blinked and we were at the hospital, which makes since, because I closed my eyes and fell asleep as soon as I sat down."

"Yo!" Hallman shouted. "We're here."

"We stumbled into the emergency room. An old lady was working at the front desk."

"Excuse me," I continued. "I think my jaw is dislocated.

"When she glanced up, her eyes widened. It must have been the amount of blood on my hand, shirt, etc. She quickly turned around, ran inside a different rom, and returned in a matter of seconds with a bag for me to spit the blood in."

"Thanks," I said.

"I could tell this hospital was on top of their game. I was still feeling no pain, quite the opposite, actually. I thought everyone might have been over-reacting and that my injury was actually no big deal."

"What happened?" she questioned.

"I got blind-side punched at a bar," I lied. "I think I was dancing with someone's girlfriend on accident. I didn't see who threw the punch."

"Oh, my," she responded. "Please have a seat over there and we'll get you back for x-rays in just one moment."

"Five minuets later, Hallman and I stumbled back into an examination room. A new, younger, attractive nurse accompanied us to this room. She was probably 35-45. It didn't take her long to notice how drunk we were."

"How did y'all get to the hospital?" The nurse asked.

"A taxi," I said.

The new examination room had two hospital beds. The nurse allowed Hallman to sleep in the second bed. He went out like a rock.

"What's your name?" The nurse questioned.

"I'm Beau."

"Well, Beau," Nurse Kent continued, "we're going to get you all fixed up."

"Nurse Kent left the room and I stayed, spitting blood. I spit blood for almost an hour before being called back into the x-ray room. The machine made a ridiculous amount of noise all around my head. I wasn't into it at all. I clenched my fists in anger. My readiness to get out of the machine rapidly grew. I held tight, though, and eventually, it was over."

"Well, Beau, your jaw is broken in three separate locations," the Doctor said as he pointed out the locations on an x-ray.

"They told me that Friday would be the earliest day that I could have my jaw wired shut.

"I bet Friday was pretty miserable for you, too." Arno said.

"It was, indeed. That Friday, my sister drove me to Dr. Jackson's office. I was the first appointment of the day at 8 a.m. After few brief tests, I went into the room where my jaw was to be wired shut. A nurse strapped laughing gas to my nose. Dr. Jackson explained that after the anesthetic, I would be responsive during the surgery, but I would not be aware of what I was saying," I continued. "When I woke up, I was confused. I saw the two nurses and Dr. Jackson in the room. I felt tired. When I attempted to yawn, my whole world came crashing down. It was the worst feeling that I had ever experienced. Yawning and sneezing were out of the question from that point on, and the next three months of food came through a straw."

"Any small victories?" Arno asked.

"Well, after two months of nothing but liquid meals, my sense of smell was sharp. I was able to smell steak and crab legs from miles away."

Arno laughed. He stood up and started to walk out.

"Alright, Beau, I'll send the doctor over tomorrow. I'll bring your beer and sandwich over either tomorrow night or the morning after."

"Try for tomorrow, I'm fucking starving already. I'd even drink a milkshake."

"No, Beau - always keep your word. Fuck milkshakes. Don't forget that."

"You're right," I continued. "Fuck milkshakes."

Chapter XIV

BLENDED POT ROAST

The next day was going to be a good day. I was going to eat a sandwich and drink good beer. That's a recipe for a success. It reminded me of the day my jaw got unwired for the first time. The moment that the oral surgeon was finished unwiring, my jaw fell open. I had not used my jaw muscles in three months, so I had a tough time closing my mouth. However, seeing as how my jaw had been locked shut for a while, I didn't find this to be a big deal. I just left it hanging open. It was a nice change.

I drove home and found that Winnie had dropped off one of my favorite foods - twice-baked potatoes. These twice-baked potatoes were not only incredible, but seeing as how I still couldn't chew, they were clutch, too. They were exactly what I needed, exactly when I needed them. I walked outside, smoked a joint and then returned to the kitchen. I threw four potatoes on a plate and tossed them in the microwave. When they were ready, I sat the first spoonful on my tongue. It was too hot, but I didn't regret it.

BAM!

The basement door swung open and the lights turned on. However, I quickly noticed that there was only one person coming downstairs. It was Arno. If there's a bright side, he's carrying a drink tray with multiple cups, along with a plastic bag with something inside.

"What do you have there, Arno?" I said through the wires on my teeth.

"I've got a vanilla milkshake, a protein drink and blended pot roast."

"Not exactly an oral surgeon, sandwich and beer..."

"I know, I'm sorry. I feel bad. I've put Johnny on locating our Doctor friend, but so far, no luck."

"What a surprise. I'd be willing to bet that Johnny knows where he is, but he's just not in a very big rush."

"Not possible. He'll be here."

"I'm sure he will be," I said with a hint of sarcasm.

Arno ignored me, "Now, do you remember what happens if I untie you and you try something funny?"

"You fuck me up?"

"Exactly. So, if you don't do anything stupid, I'll untie you so you can drink this stuff."

"Deal," I continued. "By the way, who made the blended pot roast?"

"I did. I just added some milk."

"Nice."

Milk would probably make it better than half-and-half, anyway. The unhealthier, the better. He untied my right hand and gave me the pot roast first. I took a big sip. It reminded me that blended pot roast is actually pretty good. It's basically like pot roast soup broth. You can taste every ingredient of it, but you don't have to chew. I'm not a fan of my jaw being wired shut, but if there's a bright side, it's got to be the blended pot roast. I finished the cup in about three minutes and went onto the vanilla milkshake.

"So what's in the bag?" I asked.

"It's a sandwich. I'm hungry too...do you mind?"

"You're going to sit there and eat a sandwich in front of me after you promised me a sandwich and beer?"

"I know, I know," he continued. "Having said that, you're being tortured - so deal with it."

With that, I shut up and drank my milkshake. Arno removed his sandwich from the bag. However, most likely due to the random burst of anger he had a moment earlier, he attempted to unroll his sandwich from the wrapping too quickly. It spun from the wrapper and fell to the floor. Arno frantically tried to grab the sandwich, so much so that he tipped his chair over and fell to the floor.

"Goddammit!" He yelled. He looked at the sandwich one last time before looking away in defeat. He picked up the chair, stood up and sat back down. Normally, I would have laughed, but in this particular situation, I realized that laughing might not be the wisest of moves. I doubt anyone on this planet would be in a position to laugh at Arno after he *and* his sandwich fell to the floor. Maybe his wife or kids, but that's about it...

"It's still good, Arno. No question," I reassured him.

"Are you kidding me, Beau? It's been well over five seconds by now."

"You play the five-second rule game?"

"It's not a game to me."

"I always just pick up whatever I dropped and say five seconds...regardless if it's been longer than five seconds or not."

"Well that just defeats the whole purpose of it."

"I don't know, Arno. I mean, what's the difference between, say, five and seven seconds."

"Two seconds," Arno quickly answered.

"How much dirtier could a sandwich possibly get in two seconds."

"Two seconds can make a big difference, Beau. A lot of dust particles can land on a sandwich in two seconds. I don't want to eat a dust sandwich...do you?"

"I would demolish that dust sandwich right now."

"Even now? Keep in mind, it's been sitting there for a good 30 to 40 seconds now. That's way too far past five seconds. I couldn't let you do that to yourself."

"I don't give a fuck about the dust particles. This floor is flat. If the sandwich fell on a slanted surface and rolled downhill for 40 seconds, then no, I would not eat it. But it's just been sitting in one spot this whole time. If I woke up tomorrow with my hands free, and that sandwich was still sitting there, I would eat it before I escaped."

"You wouldn't just hit a burger spot somewhere when you got out?" Arno asked.

"I probably would, but I'd eat that sandwich, too. That thing looks awesome, what is it?"

"It was a steak and cheese."

"It still is. Please go throw that thing in the blender with some milk. I'll crush it."

"If you don't die down here, you're going to die from some type of food poisoning, I guarantee it," Arno said.

"I don't think so. I'd argue that because I eat so much stuff that is considered 'dirty,' my stomach is now immune to everything. You should start eating dirty stuff to toughen your stomach up."

"He stared at it for a second, and then focused back on me.

"You think I should?" Arno asked.

"Absolutely. I guarantee that it will still taste awesome."

He continued to stare blankly at the sandwich.

"It will be a rush," I said.

Arno grabbed the sandwich and took a big bite. It was much too big of a bite to be able to keep his mouth closed while he chewed. He took another massive bite of his sandwich. It took him about a minute to finish chewing this one, which, politely, he did before speaking again.

"So, why don't you have any kids, Beau?" He asked.

"Because I'm smart," I responded.

"I have kids, Beau. Does that make me stupid?"

"No, because you're a true family man, and you've also got plenty of money," I said.

"So you're smart because you're broke with no kids."

"More or less," I responded.

"That's the most ridiculous thing I've ever heard. A smart man would want to have a child. You could teach them all the good you've learned in your life and prevent them from experiencing the bad. Having a kid is almost like having a second life and being able to live on after you're dead," said Arno.

"That's a lot of responsibility while alive, though. An expensive responsibility, too," I said.

"It's a noble responsibility, Beau."

"Maybe you're right," I continued. "But it doesn't really matter, now, does it?"

"Why wouldn't it?"

"Well, looking at my current situation, I'd say that I'm not in much of a position to be having children right now. I fucked up...what can I say?"

"Don't be so sure, Beau," he continued. "You fucked up, but who knows what will happen?"

"What do you mean?" I questioned.

He didn't answer. He took another big bite out of his sandwich, smirked and then stood up to leave.

"I'll have that doctor down here tomorrow, Beau. I promise."

"And the sandwich and beer?" I asked.

"Of course," he said.

"And what'd you mean?"

"Finish up," Arno said.

After I finished, he tied me back to the chairs, and headed up the stairs. Dammit. There was no way I would be able to sleep now. Was he just fucking with me? Was this all part of the torture? Did he want to give me hope just so he could

crush my soul? Was I really going to get that sandwich? I was so confused, and

there's nothing worse than a confusing remark combined with a smirk when you're

already confused. Arno was winning the game of torture.

Chapter XV

THE RIDE ALONG

Friday...

Winnie landed at JFK and headed straight for the police station. When she learned that no progress had been made on Beau's case, she became agitated. She began to relentlessly pressure the NYPD into stepping up their efforts.

"It doesn't look like there are any new updates, Winnie," Sgt. Mike Vaughn said.

"How can that be?" Winnie questioned.

"Finding a missing person in New York City isn't that easy of a task, ma'am."

"But I reported this on Tuesday. No progress at all has been made at all?"

"I'm sorry, ma'am. I know this can be a stressful time."

"You don't look too stressed, dear. Why aren't you out there looking for my Beau?"

"Because my job is to work at the front desk. We have some of the finest police detectives in the world here, ma'am. I'm sure they're doing everything in their power to locate your grandson."

"If y'all were the finest detectives in the world, some progress would've been made," Winnie said impatiently. "Listen to what I'm saying. My grandson is missing in your city, and nobody here seems to care!"

"We do care ma'am, but we have around 10,000 missing persons reported in New York City every year. There are a lot of worried grandma's out there."

"Are you jeering me, dear?" Winnie asked. She was beginning to lose her temper, which was very rare.

"No ma'am, not at all. I'm just trying to show you the big picture."

"So your 'big picture' is that so many people go missing in your city that it's pointless to look for one of them?" Winnie questioned.

"No ma'am, but..."

"Excuse me, miss, I couldn't help but overhear the conversation. I'm Detective Hannah Hunt."

"Hi," Winnie said, flustered. "I'm Paula Allen. You can call me Winnie. My grandson, Beau, is missing, and nobody seems to care."

"Hi, Winnie," she said. "I know how stressful this is. I'll tell you what - I just closed a case myself. How about I personally go over to Beau's place right now and look around. Where does he live?"

"I have the address," Winnie continued. "So I'll show you where it is."

"I'm sorry, ma'am, I'm going to have to insist that I do this alone," Detective Hunt responded.

"Nonsense, dear. I'm going to make sure things get done. I won't take no for an answer."

She could tell by looking in Winnie's eyes that she was going to be involved in the process, regardless of what anyone said, so she obliged.

"Okay, Winnie," Detective Hunt said.

"Detective," Sergeant Vaughn interrupted. "That's against regulations."

"Sergeant Vaughn, I'm simply taking Winnie on a ride-a-long. It happens all the time."

With that, Detective Hannah Hunt and Winnie left for Beau's apartment in Brooklyn. When they arrived, the landlord unlocked the door.

"My poor baby. I just pray that he's safe. It makes me sick to my stomach to think that he's been missing for this long," Winnie said as they entered the apartment.

"We're going to find Beau and bring him home safely to you, Winnie," Detective Hunt replied.

"Do you typically find the majority of missing persons?"

"The NYPD is the best police department in the world. If anyone can find Beau, we can," she continued. "Sit tight for a few minutes, Winnie. I'm going to browse around the apartment and see if I see anything is out of the ordinary."

Beau, surprisingly, kept his apartment in immaculate condition...outside of the marijuana paraphernalia that he left in plain sight. Detective Hunt searched the place. She ignored the non-pertinent items. Nothing seemed to be out of order, until she arrived in Beau's bathroom, where she found his phone floating in urine. She took a picture of the phone in the toilet, put on a plastic glove, retrieved the phone and dropped it into an evidence bag. She took the glove off and disposed of it before walking back into the living room.

"I found Beau's phone, Winnie."

"Where was it, sweetie?"

"It was in his toilet."

"In his toilet?

"Yes ma'am."

"Oh, dear," Winnie said worriedly.

"It's not necessarily a bad thing, Winnie."

"How so?"

"Well, there were no signs of forced entry or struggle in the apartment, only the phone floating in the toilet. It could have been an accident," Detective Hunt said.

"Don't you think he would have picked it out of the toilet, dear?" Winnie asked.

"He might have. But I also have another theory," she replied.

"Please tell, sweetheart."

"Well, this is just my opinion, but he has quite a few marijuana pipes in here," she continued. "It leads me to believe that he might have been high when he dropped the phone into the toilet. He probably thought too hard about it, and simply determined that it was too gross to retrieve," Detective Hunt continued. "I think our most logical move is to pull Beau's phone records and text messages. They'll probably give us some really good information as to where he was going,"

"That's smart. I feel much better with you on the case now, Sweetheart."

"Well thank you very much, Winnie."

"Are you married, sweetie?" Winnie asked.

"Yes ma'am, I am," she replied as she showed her wedding ring to Winnie.

"How wonderful," Winnie said with a smile. "If you had said 'no' I was going to try and fix you up with my Beau. Deep down he has a wonderfully kind soul."

"Well once we find him, I'm sure a lovely woman will snatch him right up," Detective Hunt assured Winnie.

"You're sweet to say that, dear."

"Let's head out of here, Winnie. I'll drop you off at your hotel."

"That's not necessary, dear. I'd like to stay close throughout the search."

"And you will, but you need to get some rest. After I drop you off, I'll head back to the station. I'll drop the phone off and they'll pull the records. It normally takes a day for the results to come in. I'll pick you up as soon as they I receive them.

"Okay, dear," Winnie said a tad impatiently.

They left the apartment. The investigation had legs.

Chapter XVI

BEAU ALLEN...JR.?

I didn't sleep a wink that night. How was I supposed to? One minute, I had accepted the fact that I was going to die, and the next minute, I had a glimmer of hope. I didn't know what to think.

I felt like I was on trial, the prosecutors were pushing for the death penalty, and the verdict was being revealed the next day. I would sleep horribly that night. They shouldn't tell prisoners when the verdict is being revealed. Just surprise them that morning. No one should have to face that kind of news on a bad night of sleep, yet, chances are, damn near every one of them do.

I think I'd prefer the death penalty to life in the general population of a prison. On death row, I would get my own cell and I wouldn't have much interaction with other prisoners. That means that I wouldn't have a chance to piss off a murderer or have a rapist for a cellmate. Plus, it normally takes about 20 years to actually execute someone on death row - maybe longer. There would be absolutely nothing to worry about for those first 19 years. I would pretty much just hang out the whole time, and then I'd die on a date that I would be able to mentally prepare for. I'd finally have time to write that book I've always talked about. In general population, you can get stabbed to death on any given day. It's no contest for me, death penalty all the way. The only exception would be if I were the top dog in prison. The boss. Prison wouldn't be that bad if you ran the show...

How should I handle this situation? How should I behave, now? Should I kiss Arno's ass? Maybe I should just stop talking completely. That way I won't say anything wrong. If he's fucking with me, and this is a torture method, there will be no more stories. Giving me hope when I shouldn't have hope - that's almost as bad as yawning and sneezing with my jaw wired-shut.

BAM!

The door opened and closed upstairs. It made me jump, probably because of the bad vibes that had been dominating my thought process. Regardless of the reason, I felt like a little bitch for flinching. The basement door opened and shut, the lights flicked on and feet stomped down the wooden steps. It was Arno and Dr. Stone. Arno was carrying a paper bag in one hand and beer in his other.

"Beau!" Greeted Arno.

"What's shakin' Arno?" I said through the wires.

"I found my Doctor friend. Beau, this is Dr. Stone."

"Nice to meet you," I wasn't sure what the exact rules of being a rat were, but I sure as hell wasn't going to say anything about Dr. Stone being the one who wired my jaw shut. Dr. Stone just gave me a nod. I'd guess that he wasn't really in the mood to discuss our previous meeting, either.

"Alright Doc, do your thing," Arno ordered.

Dr. Stone pulled up a chair along with a small side table for his tools. He pulled the lever on my chair, sending it into its reclined position. Then, rather quickly, he pulled out a pair of wire clippers and moved towards my face.

"Hold on a second here." I continued, "No anesthetic?"

"You don't need it for this procedure. There will be no pain at all," Dr. Stone responded.

"How about for shits and giggles?" I asked.

"Cut that shit out, Beau," Arno sternly interrupted. "Don't turn into a fucking needle-junkie. It's not a good look. You're better than that."

He was right. At some point, everyone has to draw a line in the sand that they just won't cross. Weed and beer are safely on the good side of my line, but I should limit myself to those two. It's a compromise...

"You're right, Arno," I admitted.

Dr. Stone worked quickly. It only took about five minutes for my jaw to be unlocked. Unfortunately, it took a significant amount of time to remove the braces from my teeth. When Dr. Stone was totally finished, I rubbed the outside of my teeth with my tongue. It was awesome. Not quite as awesome as the first time I had my jaw un-wired, but it was still pretty good. Rubbing my teeth wasn't even the best part about the first time my jaw was unwired. Cleaning the backs of my teeth for the first time in three months was. Talk about a relief.

"Hey Doc, I gotta' admit, my jaw feels better today than it did before it was wired. It feels like it's aligned perfectly. Maybe it didn't heal all the way last time."

"Glad to hear that," Dr. Stone mumbled.

"And Arno," I continued. "I gotta' thank you too. In retrospect, asking to be killed over a broken jaw would have been a terrible decision. This wasn't nearly as bad as I remembered."

Arno shook his head.

"You really are *crazy,* Beau," Arno continued. "I've seen a lot over my years - not many people would choose death over anything."

"Well, to be fair, I never actually made that choice. I might have if my adrenaline got pumping a little bit...that's normally when I make my shittiest decisions," I admitted. "But, I'm honored that you think I'm ballsy enough to choose death."

"Okay, Doc," Arno continued. "You're dismissed. I'll be in touch if I need you again."

The doctor gathered his tools and left the basement as quickly as possible. When he was gone, Arno turned back to me.

"Sandwich and beer," Arno said as he placed them on the small table in front of me.

"I'm speechless," I said as my mouth watered.

"I'm going to untie you...you know the drill."

"You know it!"

He untied me and I began inhaling the sandwich and beer.

"Okay, Beau. Let's get back to what we were talking about yesterday," he continued. "I told you that you might have more time."

"Yeah, I remember. I slept terribly because of it."

"You slept terribly because you might get to live longer? That doesn't make any sense," Arno said.

"I couldn't tell whether you were just fucking with me or not."

"Well, I thought more about it last night, and I've come up with an offer that will allow you to get out of this situation."

"Are you kidding me? Fuck yeah! I accept!" I exclaimed.

"Here's the first part of the deal. You never mention ANYTHING about this situation to anybody, and I mean fucking *anybody*! We call it 'Omertà.' It's a code of absolute silence."

"You have my word," I said while locking eye contact with him. I didn't want to glance at the ground and make him think that I was full of shit, so I started a staring contest.

"If you welch on your word, I'll chop your nuts off and let you bleed out slowly."

"I understand that," I responded.

"Give me your hand," he said as he pulled out his knife.

"Is the knife really necessary?"

"If you're going to give your oath in blood, it's necessary."

"Every person in the mafia does this when they make their oath?"

"That's right."

"Man, I feel like you guys have probably spread a lot of diseases during these oath ceremonies. I mean, what if the person getting initiated secretly had aids? It could wipe out an entire family!" I said.

"You have aids?"

"No, I don't have aids! I'm just saying, it's very possible for someone to have a serious disease, maybe without them even knowing about it."

"Trust me, none of us have aids."

"When was the last time there was an oath ceremony? Maybe you guys just don't know you all have aids yet," I suggested.

"It's been over a year," Arno answered.

"You're probably safe, then. I feel like aids kicks in faster than that."

"Would you shut the fuck up with the aids talk?" Arno asked.

"Hear me out. You're family sounds like they're all probably aids free. But, what about your rival families?"

"I don't think any of them have aids," Arno responded.

"Not yet," I said.

"What do you mean, 'not yet?'"

"I mean, what if you found an Italian gentleman with HIV, and paid him handsomely to make his way into a rival family. When he finally gets accepted, all of your rivals get aids. It's genius - if you're into killing your rivals with aids, that is."

"Well, that's actually not a terrible idea, but let's put it on the backburner, and get back to business," he ordered.

"Okay, okay," I obliged. Arno grabbed my hand and pulled it towards him. Next, he grabbed his knife and inched it toward my hand.

"I'm sure we could find an easier way to draw a bit of blood," I said.

"Don't be a little bitch, Beau," he answered.

"You're right. I swear to you that I'll take it to my grave."

"That's a given, Beau, one way or another," Arno warned. He poked my finger with the knife and then squeezed it until blood ran out. "Your blood is your bond, Beau."

"I understand."

"Here's the second part of the deal. You change your childish views on children, marry a family friend so that she can stay in the United States, have children and start a family with her."

My heart dropped to my knees. Any normal human being would have jumped all over this opportunity, but I knew that it wouldn't be possible.

"I can't do that, Arno," I said with a gulp.

"What do you mean you can't do that? Of course you can," he continued. "Now, here's what's going to happen-"

"Arno, I can't do it," I interrupted.

"You seriously prefer death over having children?" he asked.

"No."

"Well what's the problem then? You can't be *that* scared of having children...it's ridiculous!"

"I *was* petrified of having children."

"Petrified? Why are you petrified of having kids. Having children is the most amazing thing that can happen to anyone," Arno suggested.

"Well, I'm not petrified of having kids anymore."

"Perfect!" He exclaimed, "I'll set it up then."

"No, I'm no longer petrified because I can no longer have kids. Physically..."

"What? You're a young man. Of course you can still have children," he responded.

"Hypothetically, I would be able to, if I had not gotten that vasectomy when I was 25."

Arno went silent and simply starred at me. It was frightening. I had to say something.

"If it makes any difference, in retrospect, had I seen this in my future, I would not have gotten that vasectomy at 25."

Arno put his head in his hands and shook from side to side.

"What am I going to do with you, Beau?"

"I'll still marry her!" I offered.

"She's not going to want to marry someone who can't have children. She's a young and stunningly beautiful Italian woman. She wants a family."

"We could be an awesome husband/wife and great aunt/uncle combo, though."

"Fuck that," Arno ranted. "Now I have to call Isabella's mother and tell her that I can't deliver on my promise. What kind of boss am I if I can't keep my word?"

"Her name is Isabella?"

"Isabella Rossi."

I loved the name Isabella, and I've always thought Italian women were gorgeous. I was already in love.

"Arno, you CAN deliver on the promise. I'll marry Isabella, and I'll get a reverse vasectomy."

"They're reversible?" He asked.

"50/50. Sometimes it works, sometimes it doesn't. I happen to like 50/50 odds myself, though. I think we should let it ride, here."

"What if it doesn't work?"

"It'll work. I've got a Beau Allen Jr. or two in me. I can feel it."

Arno sat silent for a few moments before speaking. "I need to hear more about this vasectomy so I can think things through."

"It's a long story," I said.

"Long is better for you, Beau. You know how big I am on family. I'm extremely disappointed in how this whole thing played out today." Arno paused while staring at me. "I might have to kill you after all," he said to my face. Then he stood up and turned around to leave.

"You're going to leave me here on that note? How am I possibly supposed to sleep now?"

Chapter XVII

GREAT MINDS THINK ALIKE

I've always hated seeing someone the day after having an argument with him or her. Even if an apology occurs at the very beginning of the conversation, there's still a bit of awkwardness that lingers. When I was younger, I put a slice of pizza in the microwave for 10 minutes. I had seen my mom put pizza in the oven for 10 minutes - I figured it was the same. Long story short, the microwave blew up. I was not looking forward to seeing my mom that afternoon. This is worse than that. Worse case scenario with my mom and the microwave was being grounded. Now, it's death – the ultimate grounding.

I was dreading Arno's decision. I was losing myself in my thoughts. First, I would convince myself that after my story, Arno would let me live. Then, I'd tell myself that he's going to kill me for sure. It was exhausting. However, I decided that it was a good thing that Arno took a night to sleep on it. He had a night to prepare himself for my vasectomy story. Time tends to make everyone calm the fuck down. After a night to think about it, though, who knows? If there's one thing I've learned, it's that I want to live. Arno is basically the King who will make a ruling on that. He simply replaced the guillotine with a gun.

I'd love to be King. I've always thought about whether I'd rather be the King of England hundreds of years ago, or myself, just the average dude, in today's time. There are pros on cons for each side. If I chose the King, I'd be able to rock a sweet crown and live in a castle. I'd throw parties with turkey legs and wine on a regular basis. I would learn to sword fight really well, which I've always wanted to do, but, unfortunately, the ability to sword fight just isn't very useful in today's world.

On the flip side, I could die from the common cold. That would suck. There would be no ibuprofen or marijuana for wine hangovers. That would really suck. Jousting might be decent, but could it possibly be as entertaining as watching Michael Jordan play basketball? No chance. If I chose today's time, I'd get technology, which I'm a fan of. I'd get medicine - also pretty good. I'd get good music and good beer, no explanation necessary. I *would* say that I'd get sweet ways to travel, but I'm really not that impressed. Sure - cars, planes and trains can get the job done, but I'm ready for more than that. It's time for somebody to figure out the whole teleportation deal. When I can teleport to Paris for breakfast, flash to Philadelphia for a cheesesteak lunch and then hit Mexico for some burritos at night, I'll be sold on modern transportation. But until then...

BAM!

It was the infamous door slam. It was time. A terrible feeling crept over me. My mind switched back to the conclusion that Arno was going to kill me. One minute, I was about to have sex with an Italian woman and be set free. Now, I'm about to get murdered. I need a better filter when talking to Arno. I shouldn't have told him about the vasectomy. I would've gotten laid, and after a while of no luck getting pregnant, we'd just try again. We'd continue to do that for a while. After months of having a lot of sex without getting pregnant, he probably would have simply felt emasculated for me. He would've thought I just wasn't man enough to get the job done, and he would of let us live happily ever after. All I had to do was not mention the vasectomy. Fuck.

BAM!

The lights flicked on and Arno trotted down the stairs.

"Alright, Beau," Arno began. "I cleared my schedule today. This is an important day. It's judgment day. I'm going to listen to your vasectomy saga, and then I'm going to a decision as quickly and easily as the vasectomy procedure itself."

"I'm not sure if that's smart. Another night to sleep on it after you hear my story wouldn't be a terrible idea."

"I don't think so, Beau. I know this is a decision that I'll need to make at the drop of a dime. Whatever my initial gut instinct says is what I'll go with."

"What about the rest of the torture methods? You're just going to let me off the hook and end it early if you don't approve of the story?"

"Beau, even if I don't like your story and I have to kill you, I think that you've earned the right to a quick death. I won't torture you *at all* if your story sucks. I'll just give you one shot to the head, a clean execution style death."

"Thanks, I guess."

"You're welcome. Now, let's get on with it," Arno said.

"I could go for another sandwich and a beer to help get the story started."

"That's not going to happen today. Get started."

"Okay," I took a deep breath, let out a disappointed sigh, and began. "Keep in mind that this was right after the broken jaw incident. My parents had just moved to Midland, Texas, so, like any great 25 year-old son would do, I moved in with them. It didn't take long for me to become depressed. I felt like an idiot for not being successful. After some quality thinking time, I came to the conclusion that I probably shouldn't reproduce. I was not even close to being responsible enough to raise a human being, nor did I want anywhere close to that much responsibility on my plate. So - I told my parents that I was going to get a vasectomy."

Arno shook his head from side to side in disapproval. He already seemed pissed off.

"Naturally, they freaked out," I continued. "They made me talk to a therapist."

"They should have just smacked you on the head a few times to knock some sense into you," Arno said.

"Right? I couldn't believe my parents were making me see a therapist, either. They completely overreacted."

"That's not what I meant," Arno said.

I ignored him and kept rolling. "This was my first ever trip to a therapist. I made an appointment with Dr. Kathleen Robinson. The ad said that she was 35 years old and had been practicing psychiatry in Midland, Texas for the past five years. I figured that since she was young, there would be a chance that she would not be as shocked by my radical thoughts as a conservative 70 year-old man psychiatrist might have been."

"You should have gone to that conservative 70 year-old man for a second opinion."

"Eh, I don't think so," I said.

"Beau Allen?" Dr. Robinson's soft voice asked as the door to her office opened.

"That's me!" I answered.

"Dr. Robinson was attractive. She was tall with tan skin, dark hair and brown eyes. Her lipstick was a shade of dark maroon. She had on a gray business suit with a white shirt."

"Great!" Dr. Robinson continued. "Please come in and have a seat."

"Dr. Robinson's office was pretty stereotypical for a therapist. There was a sofa and a recliner, with only a coffee table separating them. They were both made of dark brown leather. The room had beige carpet and the walls were painted forest green. There was a bookcase that didn't have room for another book. There were random landscape paintings all over the room. She could use some originality. I plopped down on the sofa. Dr. Robinson sat in the recliner. I had no clue how to talk to a therapist. I was nervous. I decided to let her make the first move. After a moment of silence, she spoke...

"So, Beau," she began. "What's on your mind?"

"Not much."

"I understand that you've got a big life decision coming up."

"Did you design this office?" I interrupted. I wasn't quite ready to get into the heavy stuff.

"I did. Why?"

"No reason."

"That's an odd question to ask with no reasoning behind it."

"Well, to be totally honest, it's a bit bland. Pretty cliché, really."

"Many people think that what you call "bland" comforts them, because it surrounds them in a nice and calm setting," Dr. Robinson said.

"I can see that angle as well. It's just a bit too calm for me, personally."

"Are you not a very calm person?"

"Well, I don't know. I'm lazy, that's pretty close to calm. I never really lose my temper. That might be because I'm too lazy to get angry, though. I guess I'd say I'm pretty calm."

"When was the last time you lost your temper?" She asked.

"I got a bit upset when my parents disapproved of my plans for the future."

"Are you living with your parents now?"

"Embarrassingly, yes."

"How long have you been living there?"

"About a month. I'm already losing my mind."

"How do you cope with it?"

"I smoke a joint and think it out. I wonder how long this stage will last. Then, I sit back and look at the big picture. That always brings me back to reality. Living at home with my parents isn't the worst situation in the world. I could be in prison or the Army. But, I'd prefer to be successful, living on my own in an awesome apartment, with an awesome job and a girlfriend. If no girlfriend, ideally I'd be good at the whole 'bachelor' deal."

"You know what, Beau? I think a room that is a bit more hectic would suit you better. Have you done anything exciting recently?"

"No, not at all. I've been sitting in my parents' house all day every day, just being a lazy asshole."

"Maybe you need to do something to give yourself a rush. I find that when I experience a 'rush,' it tends to wake me up inside, and it allows me to find my voice. I suddenly get the confidence to have an opinion, voice that opinion and stand by that opinion. You'll feel better about yourself when you find your voice."

"I absolutely need a rush. I feel like I've slept through the last few years of my life. You know, I was skeptical about seeing a therapist at first, but now, I'm starting to change my mind."

"What makes you say that?"

"Because I agree with you. I was expecting someone to tell me that I was wrong over and over."

"Well, it's hard to tell someone that they're wrong when it's their personal opinion. Now, on the phone, I was told that there was a major decision you needed to make?"

"Indeed, I do."

"Tell me all about it."

"Okay, well, I still feel a bit uncomfortable…"

"Anything that we discuss here is completely confidential."

"Anything?" I asked.

"Almost anything. You can't tell me you're about to go commit a crime, but all non-criminal talk is confidential."

"Well, I guess some extremist might consider this a crime, but I certainly don't. To be honest, I've already decided. My parents disagree with my current view, so they sent me here, to discuss it with you. How fucked up does that sound? I need to talk with a therapist because my mindset is different than my parents'."

"It's not a terrible idea. If two sides disagree, it's common to have a third party give advice," Dr. Robinson suggested.

"I don't think I should have to come to an agreement with anyone but myself on this question. However, I am interested in your opinion, not only as a therapist, but also to get a female's perspective on the matter, other than my mother's."

"Let's get right down to it. What have you decided on doing?"

"I'm going to get a vasectomy," I said.

"A vasectomy?" She questioned. She seemed a bit taken back.

"A vasectomy," I continued. "My parents think that I should keep everything unscathed in that area. I say it's time to get snipped. If you had to go one way or the other, and my entire future depended on it, which way do you think you'd lean?"

"Well, that depends," Dr. Robinson answered.

"I'm already impressed that you didn't completely reject the idea right off the bat."

"It's an interesting question. I want to hear your thoughts on it first," she continued. "First of all, how old are you?"

"I'm 25."

"Do you have any children of your own?"

"No, thank God."

"Are you married?"

"Single as can be."

"When did you start to have these feelings about wanting to get a vasectomy?"

"That's a good question. I think subconsciously it started when I was a summer camp counselor. I was 19 and working at a camp where the kids stay overnight for two weeks at a time. I had a cabin full of 12-year olds, and let me tell you, 12 year-olds are miserable. I feel terrible for the parents of 12-14 year olds."

"And consciously?"

"That would be within the past six months. I recently had my jaw wired-shut for quite a while. It left me plenty of time to get some thinking done."

"What happened to your jaw?"

"That's a long story, I don't want to get into that. Just know that children did not break my jaw, so that's not where these vasectomy feelings are stemming from."

"Fair enough," Dr. Robinson said with a chuckle. "So, with your time to get some thinking done, you started thinking about vasectomies?"

"Not at first. At first, I started thinking about my future. I thought about where I want to be in 10 years. I started thinking about what the All-American lifestyle is supposed to be. It's necessary to have a wife and kids, picket fence around the house, work 9 – 5, play golf on Sundays and maybe have sex with your spouse a few times a week. It just doesn't seem that appealing to me. Then I started thinking deeper into it. Do I want to stay single my whole life? I don't think so. I think marriage can *potentially be a great thing, as long as one important factor stays out of the marriage. The kids."*

"The kids?"

"The kids," I continued. "It seems like every married couple thinks it's necessary to have kids. It's why the divorce rate is so high. They have kids and then they realize how hard the All-American lifestyle is. Kids are expensive. Financial problems cause an absurd amount of stress. Stress leads to frustration. The parents take out their frustration on their spouse and everything is downhill from there."

"Some people say that kids can also bring extreme joy to a marriage," Dr. Robinson said.

"I don't believe them. But that's not the only reason I don't want kids. Mainly, it's because I think that it's the responsibility that comes with kids. I don't want to have to raise another human being. That seems intense. I consistently make bad decisions, now I'm supposed to make all of the decisions for another human, too? That sounds like too much for me. After the kid is done being a baby, they're fun until they're about 12, and then they really aren't very fun again until they're older, out of the house and off to college. BUT, once they're in college, you get hit with a second wave of financial stress. I heard that it takes $500,000 to raise a kid from birth through college. Can you believe that?"

"I can. The average is around $250,000 prior to college," she replied.

"Well that's just ridiculous. Any argument you had for kids bringing extreme joy to life just flew out of the window. That's just too much money. If a married couple lasts through the initial financial stress of children, they normally end up getting

divorced during the second wave. Do you know what all you could do with $500,000? I'd rather take that money and travel the world with my wife. Not only could you travel the world, but you could do so in style."

"You talk about not wanting the responsibility that comes with another human being, but that's what marriage is. You have to live with another person as one, and it would be your responsibility to do so faithfully," Dr. Robinson pointed out.

"Very true - but the big difference there is that my wife would not be a kid," I replied.

"Do you like yourself, Beau?" She asked.

"What kind of question is that?" I countered. "Of course I do! Sure, I've done some things that I'm not proud of, but deep down, I know I'm a good person. I'm nice to everybody. I think I've developed some pretty good views on life over the years. But most importantly, in my opinion, is that I try not to be an asshole."

"Well, wouldn't you want to pass on those traits to a son or daughter of your own?" She asked.

"Don't get me wrong, I think my kid would turn out to be pretty cool, but I just don't want one. I think other experiences can be just as fulfilling. I'll just be an awesome Uncle."

"How many siblings do you have?"

"Three sisters."

"No brothers?" Dr. Robinson questioned.

"Nope."

"So the name 'Allen' ends with you?"

"That's right."

"How do you feel about that?

"I kind of dig it. I think it would be pretty sweet to be the tip of a branch on my family tree. I don't have any evidence to back this up, but I'd like to think that the majority of the tips of family tree branches were pretty interesting people. I'd like to hear their stories on how they became the tips of branches."

"But if you get married, you would share the end of the branch." Dr. Robinson said.

"Well," I continued. "I guess marriage is out of the question."

"You'll never get married because you want to be represented as the end of a branch on your family tree?"

"I'm kidding. Of course I'd share the end of a branch. Especially if I find a woman who was also planning on being a tip of a branch on her own family tree. Can you even imagine? Two branch tips sharing a single tip? I'm intrigued by the idea."

"When was the last serious relationship you were involved in?" Dr. Robinson questioned.

"Relationship?" I questioned. "It's been a while. I think the last time I genuinely cared for a girl was when I was 16 years old. It was the end of the summer and I was about to be a sophomore in high school. My girlfriend, Catherine, dumped me because she was heading to college."

"You haven't dated anyone since?"

"Not in a serious manner," I replied.

"So, in other words, it has been about nine years since your last relationship?"

"I guess when you do the math on it. Time flies. I've enjoyed being single, though."

"How strong would you say your feelings were towards Catherine? Did you love her?" Dr. Robinson questioned.

"I'm not sure if I loved her. I was pretty young. I know I was as down as I can imagine myself getting when she kicked me to the curb. I think one of the main reasons I haven't dated anyone long-term since then is because I tend to compare every girl I meet to her. I make a decision right then and there as to whether I could like them as much as I liked Catherine," I admitted.

"You compare every girl you meet to Catherine as soon as you meet them?"

"Yeah. That's probably not normal, is it?"

"It's actually very common to compare current relationships to an ex. Granted, the ex is normally a bit more recent than an ex of nine years, but still..."

"I need to get a girlfriend so I can prove to myself that I'm still capable of being in a relationship that lasts longer than a few weeks."

"No, Beau. You need to get a girlfriend if you have strong feelings for a girl. Relationships are not a game. You can't simply date a girl, acting as if you care for her, when you really don't. Having said that, being in a committed relationship can help you grow as a person."

"She was right. My time in college had really screwed up my views on relationships. Before college, I tried to get girlfriends. Once I got to college, I only aimed for the one-night stand. In fact, I was okay with never seeing the majority of those one-night stands again. I completely gave up after the 'chase' was over. This meant that the majority of my relationships had lifespans that varied in time, ranging from an hour to a month," I told Arno.

"If you had been in New York you could've just paid a pro and not had to worry about messing with young women's heads," Arno replied.

"Yeah…but I'm not into that whole prostitution thing. It just doesn't feel right for me."

"Prostitutes are just making a living. No reason to put them down."

"You're right," I said. There was no need to argue whether prostitution is right or wrong with a guy who most likely runs prostitution rings. Plus, who am I to judge someone who's simply trying to make a living? I just don't have any interest in STDs.

"What if you fall madly in love with someone and she wants children?" She questioned.

"I'll explain before I propose to her that having kids will not be possible. I'll tell her about the lifestyle that I can offer her. Traveling the world, wining and dining, with no babysitters to worry about.

"And if she denies that proposal?" Dr. Robinson countered.

"I don't know. If I can't live without her, then I'll figure something out. We'll adopt a kid…preferably one that is nearly 18. Or, maybe I'll freeze a bunch of sperm before my vasectomy. There are solutions," I answered.

"You'll freeze a bunch of sperm?"

"I don't know. I'm just throwing ideas out there. Do you have any children?"

"No, I do not."

"Married?" I asked

"No," She answered.

"That's interesting," I continued. "So you're basically living the lifestyle that I described as ideal."

"Not exactly. I've been working here for the past five years. Here is in Midland, Texas, so there's that. I still have the same car that I had in high school. It's not exactly traveling the world and driving luxury cars," she continued. "Now, let's get back to you. Are you nervous about potentially being alone one day?"

"You mean if I don't have any kids to set me up in a sweet retirement home?"

"Just in general," she responded.

"Well, sure...a little. Who isn't? At the same time, I've basically been alone for the past nine years, but I haven't felt lonely very often in that time span."

After glancing at her watch, Dr. Robinson said, "Looks like we're almost out of time. Has your decision to get a vasectomy changed at all after our discussion?"

"I'm getting the vasectomy for sure," I continued. "What's your honest opinion, though? Do you think I should do it?" I questioned.

"I think you should do it," she said.

"Really?" I questioned. I was surprised by the answer.

"Absolutely. You seem to have thought it out pretty well. Kids aren't for everybody. You have to be fully committed in order to raise a child. You aren't fully committed. If you want to live the type of lifestyle you described, then you might as well get a vasectomy."

"You're the best therapist in the game!" I said.

"Thanks, Beau."

"Just out of curiosity," I began. "Are you ever going to have kids?"

"No, I'm not," she answered.

"Why not?"

"Well, can you keep a secret?"

"Of course! Like you said, anything we say in here is confidential. That covers both of us."

"I had many of the same thoughts that you were having. I wanted to be my own person, too. So, I had the equivalent procedure done when I was 24."

"No way! That is so awesome! Do you regret it?"

"Not at all," she continued. "On that note, time is up. Good luck with your vasectomy, Beau."

"Let me tell you, Arno. Therapy helps. I left Dr. Robinson's place feeling like a crisp two-dollar bill. I couldn't wait to tell my parents that she agreed with me.

Chapter XVIII

TRAVELING LIGHT

"Let me get this straight - this therapist not only recommended a vasectomy, but she had the equivalent procedure done when she was even younger than you were?" Arno asked in disbelief.

"That's right," I confirmed.

"Your parents got conned out of their money. I'll never send my kid to a shrink so that they can fill their heads with nonsense."

"It takes a lot of hard work and studying to become a psychologist. I trusted her opinion 100%."

"Look at you. You're still gloating about it. I would've hated to have been your parents when you walked in the house with that shit-eating grin on your face," Arno said.

"I'm not going to lie, I did have a shit-eating grin on my face when I saw them. I couldn't help it. I had already won in my mind, regardless of whether or not I went through with the vasectomy."

"Hi, sweetie," my mom began. "How'd it go?"

"It was actually pretty awesome. I enjoyed having my brain picked apart," I replied.

"So, Dr. Robinson talked some sense into you then?" She questioned.

"Well, yeah, she made sense," I answered.

"Good!" My mother exclaimed.

"That's great news son!" My dad continued, "The Allen name can live on!"

"They turned to me and went in for a group hug. Once we were embracing, I figured there couldn't be a better time to tell them how it actually went," I told Arno.

"Well, not exactly, Dad," I said.

"The group-hug disassembled. My parents took a step back and looked livid.

"What do you mean, 'not exactly?'" My mom sternly questioned.

"I mean that I'm still planning on getting a vasectomy."

"What did Dr. Robinson say to you?" She asked.

"You mean I paid her good money for her to agree with you?" My dad began, "We're getting a second opinion!"

"She listened to me and agreed that if I want to pursue the life that I want to pursue, then a vasectomy wouldn't be a terrible idea."

"Fuck that," my dad yelled. "It's not happening!"

"I agree with your father! You're not getting a vasectomy! End of story! We will do absolutely nothing to contribute towards that, and we'll do absolutely everything to prevent it."

"It's not happening! Period!" My dad barked.

"It's not up to either of you. I'm 25 years old. That, and vasectomies aren't that expensive. I've researched this a bit. I can pay for it myself!"

"Get out!" My mother yelled.

"What?" I questioned.

"You heard me! Get out!"

"My father was silent. He just stared at me with his blood-red face."

"Fine!" I said as I turned towards my room to grab a bag.

"Your parents just went up a few notches in my book," Arno said.

"Well I still figured out a way to get it done."

"How long did that take you?"

"Just a few days."

"How'd you pay for it?"

"Well, I didn't have very much money, but, luckily, I'm a degenerate fucking gambler. Your words, not mine. So, naturally, I bet a vasectomy on a basketball game."

Arno paused and stared at me. He seemed shocked. I think he just now realized how serious my gambling problem was - or is.

"What do you mean you bet a vasectomy on a basketball game?"

"It's pretty self-explanatory. I bet a vasectomy on a basketball game," I repeated.

"Who the fuck would take that bet?"

"My friend Sledge's father. He also performed the vasectomy."

"What kind of sick story is this? Your best friend's old man gave you a vasectomy?"

"It's not as bad as it sounds. Sledge's Dad is a urologist in Los Angeles."

"It's still totally inappropriate. How'd you end up in Los Angeles?"

"I hitchhiked."

"You hitchhiked with all the sick fucks out there? I'm surprised you didn't end up dead in a ditch," he said.

"Well, I wouldn't have had to hitchhike, but I ran into a bit of car trouble."

"Ran out of gas?" Arno asked.

"Something like that. After my parents told me to leave, I figured that I'd drive as far as I could and then I'd figure it out from there. I grabbed a duffle bag, along with a couple pairs of socks, underwear, toothbrush, deodorant, sunglasses, shorts, jeans, phone, my fat sack of weed, my bowl, a lighter, a few condoms, car keys, and last but not least, the six doses of LSD that I had been saving for a rainy day. In my mind, it was pouring. These were my necessities."

"LSD was a necessity for you?"

"This was a weird time for me. I was freaking out a bit. I was running away so that I could voluntarily have a surgical operation done in the general vicinity of my penis. I wasn't thinking clearly, to say the least. I was looking for an answer."

"I've never done it," Arno said.

"LSD or a vasectomy?" I asked.

"Either, but I was referring to the LSD," he replied. "I've always been interested, but now I'm just too old. I should've done it in the 70s."

"As long as you're alive, you're never too old to try something new."

"You may be right, but I'm still not going to do any psychedelics."

"To each his own, I guess. Anyway, my parents had walked outside and were in the back yard. I didn't blame them for needing some fresh air after that argument, but I also didn't think a goodbye was necessary at that point. With them being outside, it also happened to be the perfect time to steal the spare change bucket from their bedroom. There was close to 300 dollars worth of quarters in it. I snuck back to their bedroom, emptied the ridiculously heavy change bucket into my bag and ran out of the front door of the house. I hopped into my Honda Civic coupe, well, your Honda Civic coupe. I figured it was as good of a time as any to get the psychedelic journey started. After all, I had a lot of thinking to do on this road trip. I reached into my bag, grabbed the LSD, and tossed two hits onto my tongue. It was go time."

Chapter XVIV

ROAD TRIPPING

"So you had a bit of car trouble after eating a bunch of LSD and attempting to drive? Shocking."

"I was a bit shocked myself," I said.

"If the LSD had nothing to do with your car troubles, then your debt is forgiven. You can get up and walk out right now," Arno offered.

I stopped to think. Should I just lie and say that it didn't have anything to do with it? Or should I just tell the truth and try to get some credit for being honest?

"Your hesitation gave it away, Beau," Arno said.

"Dammit."

"So, let's hear it. What happened?"

"Well, after cruising around for a few minutes, I decided to head for the interstate. I was still unsure of where I was heading, but interstates are straight and you can drive fast, so it seemed like a good idea. About 20 minutes had passed from the time I ate the acid to the time I got to Interstate 20. I could feel a warm body-high sneaking over me. I looked at the sign for both I-20 East and West. I-20 West had better vibes, so I decided to roll with it. The merge ramp was on the left, which looked much more challenging than a merge ramp on the right. I whipped the car to the left and onto the ramp. An orchestra of horns sounded behind me. However, there was no looking back now - only forward...only west."

"You could've killed somebody!" Arno yelled.

"You might kill me later, so what's your point?"

"You might've killed an innocent child. I might kill a degenerate gambler. Big difference," Arno said.

He wasn't wrong.

"I had a full tank of gas. My parents filled her up before my therapy appointment. They said they wouldn't contribute to my vasectomy, but a full tank of gas was clutch on my journey towards the scalpel. A few miles down the road on I-20 W, I began to feel...*tingly*. I could feel every part in the car working. The wheel seemed like it was violently shaking. It reminded me of the shitty motel beds that vibrate when you put a quarter in. I began to wonder if there was a slot in the wheel for quarters that I had never known about. How else could it the car be vibrating like it never had before? It didn't take long for me to be completely convinced that there was a vibrating quarter slot in my car. I was bewildered as to why I had never noticed. It was time to pull over and investigate. After all, I had made it almost five miles down the road - it was as good of a time as any to stop for my first break. In preparation, I got a quarter out of my center console."

"And you'd recommend this stuff?" Arno asked. "Something that just puts you out of your mind?"

"Yes," I continued. "I merged off I-20W and turned into a *Texas Express* gas station. I went to the right side of the building, where I wasn't visible to the gas station employees - it felt safe. I turned the car off, took my keys out of the ignition, took a deep breath and exhaled. I had made it, and I was feeling great. However, after about a minute, confusion crept over me. What was I doing at the gas station? I looked around the car, and then noticed that I had a quarter in my hand. I investigated both sides of the quarter, and after a moment, I realized why I had pulled over! Yes! The quarter-slot! Ok, where is this goddamn thing? There was nothing on the wheel and nothing to the left of the wheel. However, when I searched to the right of the wheel I found it. How had I not known about this until now? It must have been fate. I wasn't supposed to find it until that exact moment."

"Fate?" Arno questioned.

"That's what I originally thought, at least, but then fate was interrupted when the quarter did not fit into the slot. Talk about a curveball. A slot that was made for quarters doesn't accept quarters? I tried harder. It just needed a little elbow grease. Determined to make it work, I jammed the quarter into the slot with *power*. Yes! I began to laugh, feeling as if I had won."

"You didn't win, did you?"

"I didn't," I continued. "The first wave of an acid trip is always a little confusing. It arrives very subtlety, until you notice it. Once you notice, it heats up quickly. Most of the time, it's a visual that sets it off. It can be something as simple as looking at a picture that suddenly starts to swirl around a little bit. Next, you look at the rest of your surroundings, and you notice that everything is swirling around a little bit. Until you accept it as normal and roll with it, it'll be a little weird."

"So what happened?" Arno asked.

"Well, when my laugh died down, another wave of confusion crept back over me. I looked at my surroundings and realized I was still at the gas station. I glanced in the passenger seat and saw my keys. I thought it was a perfect time to get the hell of out there. I grabbed the keys and tried to slide them into the ignition, but that was a no-go. For some reason, the keys didn't fit. This called for another immediate investigation. I looked at the ignition closely and realized that a quarter had been jammed into it. Fuck. I grabbed the quarter and pulled, but it didn't budge. I tried again, with all my force, but my fingers had become far too sweaty, and they slipped off with ease."

"Yeah this drug sounds great," Arno said sarcastically.

"After I realized that the car was basically screwed, I had the urge for a cigarette, or 20 – so I walked into the store. The sound of the refrigerators took over my brain. They were giving off a loud, constant buzz. It was entirely too loud. I looked at the checkout counter. The clerk was staring at me. Does he know? I nodded in acknowledgement. He just kept staring. I noticed the cigarettes behind him. Jack pot. I'll settle for smokes and I'll get the hell out of here. I got to the counter and looked over the selection."

"How's it going?" I said with a nervous stutter.

"What can I get for you?" He asked.

"Umm...let's see."

"I glanced around. There were too many choices. Should I go menthol or normal? Splurge for brand name or just get whatever is cheapest? I overthought it," I told Arno.

"Sometime today," the impatient clerk said.

"Ahhhh..." I muttered, attempting to buy some time.

"Come on man, just pick one," he ordered.

"Just give me whatever you got, man," I spat out.

"Whatever I have? You want one of each? That'll be about 50 packs of cigarettes," he said.

"That's too many cigarettes," I replied. *"I'll just take one pack."*

"OK," he continued. *"Which brand?"*

"I don't know, man," I admitted in defeat. *"Can't you just pick one for me?"*

"He looked bewildered, but he turned around, grabbed a pack of smokes, and tossed them on the counter. They were *Parliaments*. P-funks. Perfect."

"That will be $4.52." He informed.

I reached behind me for my wallet, but there was nothing. Panic returned.

"I don't have my wallet," I said.

"Well I can't sell you the smokes, then," he responded.

"It might be in the car."

"That's great," he continued. *"You should go get it if you want the smokes."*

"Oh...right," I replied. *"I'll go grab it!"*

"I turned towards the door and walked outside. I could feel his eyes on me until I rounded the corner, where I took a deep breath. Whew! I had made it! It was a good time to get the hell out of there," I said.

"What about your smokes?" Arno asked.

"There was no chance I was going to go back in that store. I got back in my car and attempted to put my keys in the ignition. I had already forgotten there was a quarter jammed in the ignition. I looked around and thought about my options. It didn't take long for me to make a decision. I reached in the back and grabbed my duffle bag. I got out of the car, tossed my bag over my shoulder, and started walking. I walked about half a mile, before I realized I wanted a cigarette, so I turned around and walked back to the gas station. This time, I went in on a mission.

"One pack of parliaments, please."

"$4.52," he said.

"I dumped five dollars in quarters on the counter. The clerk wasn't too pleased with having to count them. After he counted the correct amount, he nodded, and I left.

"Sir, you forgot the cigarettes, and your change."

"Oh, shit. Thanks," I said as I walked back to grab them.

"Once again, I left on foot. After a few minutes, I opened the pack of cigarettes and pulled one out. Then, I realized I didn't have a lighter. Back to the store.

"One lighter, please," I said.

"$1.15," the attendant said. "Are you sure that's all you need?"

"That'll do," I said as I handed him more change. "Keep the change."

"I lit one up the moment I walked outside, and then, I started truckin'. Step by step, I cruised down the side of I-20W. The more I walked, the better I felt. It was like I was in my natural habitat. It was where I was always meant to be. I was thinking about only walking for transportation, for the rest of my life. I felt free.

"I am Beau, hear me roar!" I yelled into the air, before I followed it up with a series of coughs. I needed to quit smoking cigarettes.

"It felt good to yell, outside of the pain of violently coughing. Nobody could hear me. Cars were buzzing by at a million miles per hour, and as each one passed, the sound of another galaxy blew past. I eventually learned how to mimic the sound of the passing cars, and I made the noise as every car passed. It was a good time."

"Sounds like a good time," Arno joked.

"It was, until I eventually got tired of walking. Physically, I felt fine. However, my natural habitat high had worn off, and I now thought that man was meant to travel on a comfy seat with good tunes blaring. I decided to stick the old thumb out to the side and see if I could get a lift. However, I pulled my thumb in as every car passed, not out of the fear of hitchhiking, but because I was nervous that my thumb would be taken off by one of the cars that seemed to be traveling at the speed of light."

"Let me guess," Arno continued. "Not many people wanted to give a guy with a mustache a ride?"

"No, they did not. It was a tragedy. I kept walking until, predictably, an 18-wheeler pulled over about 50 yards in front of me. Fuck it. I was starting to feel confident, maybe confident enough to kick a truck driver's ass if necessary. I lightly jogged towards the truck. I wasn't sure of the proper hitchhiking etiquette, as far as how long you should take to get to the car. A 50-yard casual walk might take me a little while to complete. If I'm the driver, I'm thinking about leaving after 20 seconds. However, a dead sprint is desperate, and I'm not in the shape I was in at 18. I'd probably get a cramp halfway to the truck. I decided a light jog was probably expected in most hitchhiking scenarios - so that's what I did. When I got to the truck, I climbed up the passenger door and spoke to the driver through the open window.

"Need a lift?" The driver asked.

"Yes sir!" I yelled ecstatically.

"Hop in," he said.

"I swung the door open and hopped in. I had never been on the inside of an 18-wheeler. I felt like I was about 15 feet in the air. It was mind-blowing. I tossed my bag on the floorboard of the passenger seat."

"Beau Allen," I announced as I extended my hand in greeting.

"Hal Simmons," he slurred back at me.

"You feeling alright there, Hal?" I asked.

"Oh yeah, I'm great," he responded.

"Something wasn't quite right about this dude. I stared at him for a moment. He was a smaller guy with brown hair, a trucker hat, and a rocking mustache. This guy looked exactly like me! Was this some sort of sick, twisted joke?"

"Where'd you start walking from, Beau?" Hal questioned.

"I haven't been walking long. Only for about 15 minutes or so. I started back at the Texas Express, about 5 miles outside of Midland," I replied.

"That's about seven miles from here. You walked seven miles in 15 minutes?"

"Seven miles!" I said in disbelief.

"Shit...maybe even more," Hal replied.

"Are you fucking with me?"

"Nope," Hal slurred before following with a burp.

"What time is it?" I questioned.

"Getting close to 4 p.m.," Hal continued. "Listen, Beau, I gotta' tell you something."

"I subtly moved my hand onto the latch on my door. I needed to be ready to make a quick exit."

"I am fucked up right now," Hal admitted.

"You're what?"

"I am shit-faced...hammered...slammed."

"Really?" I questioned.

"I shouldn't be driving this thing right now. I've been pounding moonshine for the last 100 miles."

"You've been drinking moonshine for 100 miles?"

"That's right," Hal answered, as he reached behind his seat and lifted up a large, half-full Mason jar.

"Fuck," I said.

"Beau...I'm gonna' need you to drive this thing," Hal told me.

"I looked at Hal and quickly realized that he was dead serious. I know, because that's what I look like when I'm dead serious. I thought that it must have been my destiny to drive that truck," I told Arno.

"Say no more," I began. "It would be an honor!"

"Alriiiiiiight!" Hal hollered.

"He held his hand up for a high five and I connected. A beautifully connected high-five always overflows with good vibes. It was exactly what I needed before attempting such as task. Hal climbed into the back of the truck and onto his bed. I quickly climbed over the center console and into the driver's seat. Fuck yeah."

"Wait, wait, wait," Arno continued. "Now, not only are you driving on the interstate while fucked up on acid, but you're also doing it in a massive death machine! An 18-wheeler!"

"That's the thing about acid. Your mind can jump around very easily. I had already forgotten about not being any good at driving my small car. I was currently excited to drive an 18-wheeler."

"Hal, I've got to tell you, I've never even been in one of these things. I don't know the first thing about driving one. I don't even know how to drive a stick shift," I admitted.

"No worries, I'll help out with the truck. I can explain how to drive this thing in my sleep," Hal continued. *"The truck is ready to be started. Key is halfway in. There is a lever on the ground by your left foot. All you need to do is step on that leaver and turn the key forward."*

"I followed his instructions, and sure enough, the truck roared like the biggest lion in the jungle, and then started vibrating. The vibrations moved through my entire body. I started laughing, once again, to the point of crying."

"What's so funny?" Hal questioned.

"I looked at him as his words bounced around the truck and repeated themselves. 'Stay in control,' I thought to myself."

"Nothing, nothing, let's do this thing."

"Hal talked me through the steps to driving. Surprisingly, my mind grasped all of his instructions and I got it rolling!"

"So irresponsible," Arno chimed in. I ignored him and kept rolling.

"We cruised on. Hal took a few more big swigs of moonshine and passed out like a rock within minutes. Over the next 3 hours, I got into a truck-driving zone. I was listening to 1970s jams while flying high down the road. It was great. Next time I hit rock bottom, I'm going to become a truck driver. It's really not a bad gig. You can just cruise while jamming out all day every day. I was thoroughly enjoying it," I continued. "Unit I ran into a little bit of a problem. I got to the end of I-20W. It merges into I-10W and crosses into New Mexico. Hal was sound asleep. I wasn't sure if I should wake him up? I thought about how I hate being woken up shortly after I fall asleep, especially after drinking. I decided that he was probably the same way, so I let him sleep. I wondered if he is on any type of certain route right now, or if he was just hitting the open road...in his environmentally friendly 18-wheeler? Fuck it. New Mexico - Hal and I would be there soon."

"No one drives places for fun in an 18-wheeler, Beau," Arno said.

"No, they don't, Arno - but Hal was now my hitchhiker. It was his own fault for trusting a totally random person to drive his truck. Another three and a half hours blew by in a flash. Hal remained out cold."

"Hal's a fucking moron," Arno said.

"It would be tough to debate that," I replied. "My vision settled in on a green sign in the distance. As I approached the sign, I realized what it said.

"Los Angeles, CA, 700 miles."

"Wheels started turning in my head. My fraternity brother, Sledge Hill, lived in L.A. He lived with his parents because, like myself, he's messed up a few times. I know how to associate myself with good people, and anyone who can live with their parents as a total failure and not commit suicide is what I consider 'good people.' Also, Sledge's Dad is not only the man, but he's a Doctor, and not only is he a doctor, he's a fucking Urologist! Urologists just so happen to be the doctors who perform vasectomies. I couldn't believe that I hadn't thought about this earlier. I had met Sledge's Dad when he came to visit Sledge during our sophomore year - well, our second year of college. We were both still freshmen, technically. We called Sledge's Dad the Condovian Space Snake. The night he visited, he partied harder than any student on campus. Now, it wasn't totally his fault that he partied all night. After we convinced him to smoke a joint with us, we figured it was fair game, so we spiked his drink with molly while we were at the bar."

"What's molly?" Arno asked.

"It's basically pure ecstasy," I told him.

"You spiked a doctor's drink with ecstasy?"

"I figured he could thank me later," I said.

"I must admit," Arno continued. "That's the one drug I've always wanted to try. I hear that sex is supposed to be incredible on it."

"It is, Arno...it is."

"Do you know of anyone who sells it in New York?" Arno asked.

"You're the one who runs the underground scene in New York."

"I don't want my guys to know that I'm getting fucked up on hard drugs," Arno said.

"First of all, it's not that hard of a drug. Second, if they ask, just tell them that it's for a date night with you and Mrs. Arno. Third, who gives a fuck what they say? You're the boss!"

"You're right...but I still don't want to ask them," Arno admitted. "So, did Sledge's father enjoy himself?"

"Enjoy himself? He loved it. He went on to blow every person's mind in the bar with his dance moves. At the end of the night, Sledge's father had earned the nickname, the Condovian Space Snake. It fit like a glove. So – after I saw the sign, I decided I'd head to L.A. and see if Condovian could hook me up with a cheap vasectomy."

"That was your plan?"

"That was the plan. It seemed like a good one at the time."

"It wasn't."

"How do you know? I haven't got to that part yet."

"Because I'm not a moron."

"Do you want me to continue the story?" I asked sarcastically.

"Watch your tone," Arno ordered. "Now, continue."

"Well, after I had my plan, I zoned in on the road, and soon enough, I was experiencing pretty extreme tunnel vision. This meant that there would be no warning call to Sledge - or to his parents. I had to focus."

"This sounds absurdly dangerous for so many people," he said.

"Sorry boss," I continued. "Every time I saw a mileage update, it blew my mind again. It seemed like every time I saw a sign that said "Los Angeles," I was 100 miles closer than I was before. However, the fun came to an abrupt stop when I realized the truck needed gas. I was going to have to make a turn. Fuck. I blew past 16 exits before I finally worked up the courage to merge onto the exit. Once I did, I realized it was much easier than I had originally thought it would be. I pulled into the gas station, put the truck in park and turned it off."

"Hal!" I yelled.

"There was no sign of life from him."

"Hal!" I tried again.

"Once again, he didn't move. For a moment, I thought that Hal might be dead. Horrible thoughts raced through my mind. This would not be a good situation if I were driving Hal's truck while he's dead in the back. I don't know how I would explain that. I decided that if he's dead, I'm stealing his identity, and allowing him to live on. It was time for a moment of truth. It was time to check for a pulse. I leaned back and pressed my fingers on his neck. *Thump, thump. Thump, thump. Thump, thump.* I thought about the weirdness of the human body. Hearts pumping blood, having random spots on your body where your heart beat can be felt. *Thump, thump. Thump, thump.* After about 15 seconds, I realized that this wasn't a science experiment. I was checking to see if Hal was alive. Then I realized the *thumps* meant that he was indeed alive. Talk about a relief."

"I honestly thought you were going to tell me that Hal was dead," Arno said.

"I saw Hal's wallet on the dash. I figured that his company would probably reimburse him for gas. I opened his wallet and removed his credit card. I opened the driver's door and looked down. I forgot how high up these trucks are. I've always been a bit scared of heights as well. I bravely climbed down. I was relieved when I got to the ground. I walked over to the pump and stared at the digital screen. The numbers flew around, making it impossible to read. This was going to be difficult. I slid the credit card in and pulled it out. The words, "Zip Code?" floated around on the screen. *Fuck.* What now? My brain started clicking...I had his wallet! *Clutch.* I opened his wallet and grabbed his driver's license. He was from Little Rock, AR, 72201. Perfect. I punched in 72201, and sure enough, the card was accepted. I gave a subtle fist-pump and then got down to business. I hooked the hose up to the truck and let it flow..."

"How much did it cost to fill that thing up? I've always been curious," Arno said.

"A few hundred. The gas tanks on those trucks must be huge. It took forever for the nozzle to automatically stop. Let's just hope they reimbursed him," I answered.

"Hal!" I yelled again.

"I cranked the truck up, using the same steps that Hal had told me earlier, and put it into gear. Off we went. I merged back onto the interstate like a champ. I only had 400 more miles until Los Angeles. I'm hoping I don't have to fill up the tank again before L.A. My buzz wasn't feeling as strong as before. I still had five and a half hours to go. I couldn't think of a better time to eat my last four hits of acid. I reached in my bag, grabbed them and put them under my tongue. Now, it was go time - again. After a few miles, my tunnel zone intensified. The miles flew by. The signs started appearing faster and faster. With 300 miles left, the colors were bright, and my long distance sight was better than ever. With 200 miles left, everything seemed to turn into a moving visual effect. At one point, I glanced down and noticed that the denim in my jeans was moving in wild, circular patterns. I decided it was best to ignore it and stare at the road."

"Good call," Arno said.

"With 100 miles left, I was in completely comfortable with the acid. Nothing could have startled me. I could have apologized to my parents with confidence if necessary. I could make patterns hallucinate, or I could ignore them completely. The radio's music bounced around the background of my attention span beautifully, while the foreground of my attention span was locked in on the road. Everything was great, until I had 50 miles to go."

"What happened?" Arno asked.

"I noticed intense colors out of my peripheral vision. At first, this just made me feel like I was at a rave, so I grooved a little bit with the music. Then, a terrible feeling landed in the pit of my stomach. Something was wrong. I became paranoid. I felt like someone was watching me. I glanced around in every direction. The second my eyes set on the side-view mirrors, I knew exactly what was wrong. A cop's blue lights were flashing. It was the five-o. I thought I was completely fucked.

I turned the music all the way off, thinking that I needed silence to think. However, when the music went silent, I quickly changed my mind. Silence is not a good thing while tripping. A little background noise always helps to calm the situation."

"So, what'd you do?" Arno asked…

"I pulled over, rolled down my window, turned the engine off - but left the battery rolling. I needed to have a soundtrack for this particular moment. I turned the volume up a bit. The Grateful Dead's 'I Need a Miracle' ironically flowed through the truck, and then Hal woke up.

Chapter XX

THE FIVE-O

"Beau, what's going on?" Hal questioned as he rubbed his eyes and stretched.

"Hal!" I whispered, "Give me your hat!"

"What?"

"Give me your fucking hat, lie back down and don't say a fucking word," I ordered.

"What the fuck is going on?" Hal asked again as he handed me his hat.

"A cop. I've got this," I said as I turned around, slid the hat on and shot him a confident wink. "Here he comes - total fucking silence!"

The officer was walking slowly. The first thing I noticed was his mustache, which led me to believe that I might be able to talk my way out of this. After all, I also had a mustache. I grabbed Hal's wallet and mentally prepared. As soon as the officer was close to the door, I spoke.

"Is there a problem officer?" I asked.

My depth perception was off. The officer didn't hear me. He was still a good 40 feet from the driver's door of the truck. Everyone is better with a practice round, anyway.

"Is there a problem officer?" This time the officer heard me.

"License and registration please," the officer answered emotionlessly.

My heart sank. I forgot that he would ask for my registration. I didn't have a clue where it could possibly be, until I glanced down by my side and realized how legendary Hal Simmons was. His outstretched hand had his registration card in it. Slyly, I grabbed the card. Next, I slid Hal's driver's license out of his wallet and handed them both to the cop."

"Here ya' go," I said.

"He stared at the license, and then looked at me. He looked back at the license for a moment, and then the registration card. Then, he handed them both back to me."

"You were going a little fast back there, Hal," the cop informed.

"Was I?" I continued. *"I'm sorry about that, I've been driving for a while and had gotten in a bit of a rhythm with the flow of traffic. I'll watch my speed closely from here on out."*

"The police officer either had a suspicious look on his face. I could feel my face turning red and sweat gathering on my forehead."

"Where are you headed?" The police officer asked.

"Los Angeles...all the way from Texas!"

"What are you transporting?"

"Naturally, I had absolutely no clue what we were transporting. For all I know, Hal could have been the biggest drug mule in America, and the trailer was packed to the brim with cocaine."

"You know, I'm not really sure. I just focus on the driving. I'll be glad to open her up if you need me to, though," I said.

"I prayed that he would say he didn't need to. I didn't have a fucking clue how to open a trailer. That would've been a dead giveaway. The cop took a moment to respond while he weighed his options."

"No, that's alright. I'm not going to prolong your day after a drive like that. Watch your speed. You're almost to L.A. Get there and take a nap."

"Will do!" I said. "Thanks, officer. I appreciate it."

"I climbed back up into the driver's seat, where I stayed completely silent until the pig got in his car and drove off. Hal did not."

"Un-fucking-believable!"

"His celebration made me jump. I had forgotten that Hal was back there. I thought I was Hal. That must be how method actors feel when filming ends. I seemed to be having a strong wave of the acid."

"Now, where are we?" Hal questioned.

"Almost to L.A."

"L.A.?" Hal asked before bursting into laughter.

"Is that a bad thing?"

"Fuck no! That was my destination. I successfully got shit-faced drunk, passed out on the job and woke up where I was supposed to be. Beau Allen...I can't thank you enough. You saved my ass!"

"No way!" I said before joining in on his laughing attack. Eventually, I gathered myself. "You have to drive this thing now, Hal. It's a miracle we're not dead from the first part of the drive," I stated.

With that, I climbed back over the center console and into the passenger's seat. That had been quite a journey. Hal climbed into the driver's seat. We only had fifty miles left until Los Angeles. After a fist bump, and turning the 70s tunes back on, it was time to cruise. I would be at Sledge and Condovian's in no time. From there, my only worry would be talking the Condovian Space Snake into giving me a vasectomy - preferably on the house.

Chapter XXI

MARCH MADNESS

"No doctor is going to give a guy a free vasectomy," Arno said.

"What makes you so sure of that?" I questioned.

"I'm sure they don't necessarily enjoy working with scrotums. They only do it because it pays the bills 10 times over."

"Well, I felt like Condovian and I were good friends - great friends, in fact - despite only meeting once. If any doctor was going to give me a free vasectomy, it would be him."

"What did he say about your absurd offer?"

"Well, when I banged on door, Sledge opened it and stood in front of me. He was confused. His head tilted to the side, like a dog trying to understand its owner."

"Beau?" He questioned.

"Is that a question?" I responded.

"Kind of. What are you doing here?" Sledge asked as he moved in for a bear hug.

"We'll get to that," I responded as the bear hug broke. "More importantly, what are you doing answering the door?"

"What?" Sledge said. "I live here."

"Dude, I never answer the door or the phone at my parent's house," I said.

"That's because you're a lazy asshole," Sledge informed me.

"It has nothing to do with being lazy. It's pretty much all about being an asshole," I continued. "When someone knocks on the door of my parents house, or calls, it's most likely for my parents. Not for their 25 year-old son who they thought was out in the world being successful," I said.

"You thought I was out in the world being successful?" Sledge asked.

"Well, no, not me personally, but the average parent's friend doesn't know everything about each others' kids…maybe their age. When they hear the age 25, they aren't expecting them to answer the door of their parent's house," I responded.

"Yeah, but you knew I lived here," Sledge said.

"I realize that, but you shouldn't answer the door, because outside of this one time, the door is never going to be for you."

"What?" Sledge asked, "Are you fucked up right now?"

"No, why? Am I not making sense?" I asked.

"Not at all, and your pupils are taking up the majority of your eyeballs," Sledge answered.

"That's weird," I said as I picked up my bags and walked past Sledge into his parent's house. I paused next to him and said, "Maybe it's because I ate six doses of acid on my way here," I said quietly. "Oops! Now, where are your fantastic, loving, understanding, ready to accept me as their own parents of yours?" I asked loudly.

"I walked around the corner where I could hear a basketball game blaring from the television. Sports Broadcasters sound super intense on psychedelics. Their voices tend to echo and they're always entirely too excited. Sledge followed me, nervous as to what I might say to his parents. I saw Condovian's head staring at a television, and felt the urge to drown the broadcaster's voices out with my own. I needed to make the Space Snake aware of my presence," I told Arno.

"CONDOVIAAAAAAAAAAAAN!" I yelled at the top of my lungs.

"Goddammit!" Condovian yelled. "You scared the shit out of me, Beau."

"I'm sorry, Condovian," I continued. "I couldn't help myself. It's not every day that I get to see my favorite Urologist!"

"Sledge's father turned and gave me a hug."

"What brings you to L.A.?" Condovian asked.

"Sledge invited me," I said with a wink in Sledge's direction. "No, I'm kidding. I'm a gypsy on the move now and I just kind of found myself in L.A. But in all seriousness, if I could crash here for a could of days, that would be unbelievably clutch."

"Of course, Beau. Stay as long as you need," Condovian hesitated. "Or - at least for a few days."

"That's incredible! Thank you so much," I said. "Where's Mrs. Hill at today?"

"Mrs. Hill is vacationing in Europe with some of her girl friends for the next week. You caught us at the right time. It's man week at the Hill house. Nothing but pizza, beer and March Madness," Condovian said.

"I felt like I was dreaming. After my road trip shenanigans, I couldn't imagine anything better than pizza, beer, a couch and not having to act sober in front of Sledge's mom. She had a keen eye for someone being fucked up – probably because she's had so much practice with Sledge. The basketball tournament was purely a bonus. I knew it wouldn't be exciting enough to keep my current state of mind occupied, though. We needed to make the game interesting, and I had just the thing."

"Have a seat and indulge," Condovian invited.

"You don't have to tell me twice." I continued, *"Who's playing?"*

"ESPN is showing Duke vs. Weber State. It's the 16 seed versus the 1 seed. This one is a blow out," Condovian said.

"You mind if we throw some tunes on in the background instead of listening to the commentators, Dad?" Sledge asked.

"Go for it, but don't play any of that new crap," Condovian answered.

"Condovian sounds like a smart man. Some of the new stuff that you kids call music is terrible," Arno said.

"I agree that there is a lot of terrible new stuff out there, but we have some phenomenal musicians as well. It's different. But, overall, I'm with you. I dig the 60s and 70s tunes. I also like the big band music of the 20s, jazz, The Rat Pack, the blues of the 50s, some of the classic rock songs from the 80s. I loved the 90s hip-hop, and I think the jam bands of today are incredible."

"You like the Rat Pack?" Arno asked.

"Of course! I do my best Sinatra impression in the shower almost daily," I answered.

"Me too," Arno replied.

"Anyway, Sledge glanced at me and nodded. He had tried LSD before, so he knew that music is infinitely better than a sports broadcasters' crazy voice. Combining music with either sports or the nature channel during the trip is always a good time, too. There's not much better than watching a lion hunt to Led Zeppelin. Sledge plugged his Grateful Dead mix into the surround sound speakers. It was perfect."

"Beau, you want a beer?" Sledge asked.

"Sledge, that's two big time developments in a row. You're on a roll. Yes, I will take a beer."

"So, Beau," Condovian continued. "What are you up to these days?"

"I'm in a little bit of a transitional period right now," I answered.

"I know what you mean. Sledge has been teaching me about the importance of these transitional periods," Condovian said.

"You've got a good teacher for that subject," I said.

"Sledge returned from the fridge with three Pale Ales. He handed one to Condovian and me."

"Good beer!" I said.

"Of course it's good beer. Good beer is one of the keys to happiness in life." *Condovian preached. "A good beer after a hard day's work is euphoric. A good beer without having to work is even more euphoric. I can't even taste light beers anymore."*

"Preach. An IPA is the equivalent of a small amount of Xanax and a light beer. I'm normally slammed after six of them," Sledge said.

"Well...cheers then, boys." Condovian said.

"So, Condovian," I began. "Have you burned one since the last time I saw you?" I asked.

"Not really," Condovian continued. "Maybe twice since I visited you boys a while ago."

"We should do something about that," I replied.

"I'm not opposed at all!" Sledge chimed in.

"I'm sure you're not, Sledge," Condovian said. "That would be about your fourth smoke session of the day."

"What's wrong with that?" Sledge asked. "I thought it was man week. Take a toke."

"Well, twist my arm," Condovian continued. "Let's do it."

"I reached into my bag and pulled out the weed. It was close to an ounce," I told Arno.

"Jesus!" Condovian said.

"It's Beau, Condovian," I replied.

"I thought it was Beau Allen?" Sledge chimed in.

"Whoa," I said with a temporarily blown mind. Names were echoing.

"That's a lot of weed!" Condovian observed.

"It is indeed, Condovian," I continued. "I may not be good at much, but I've always been good at finding a big bag of weed."

"Yes he has!" Sledge said.

"I quickly twisted a joint and handed it to the space snake."

"Here you go, Condovian, chief away," I said.

"You know, I think I'd smoke more often if I had that quality and quantity of weed. Not bad...not bad at all," Condovian admitted.

"You want this bag of weed?" I asked Condovian.

"How much?" He replied.

"I'll put it on the line during the next good basketball game," I proposed.

"I'm interested. A little gamble always spices things up in sports. Especially now that I've got a buzz going," Condovian said. "How much?"

"I'll tell you what, you don't even have to put a specific number on the line," I said.

"I don't know what that means," Condovian replied.

"Me either, Dad," Sledge said.

"You put a vasectomy on the line," I said.

"What?" Condovian questioned with a laugh. "I've already had a vasectomy. As soon as I had Sledge I got snipped," Condovian said.

"I'm not talking about for you. If you win the bet, I give you the bag of weed. If I win the bet, you give me a vasectomy," I offered.

"What? Fuck that, that's insane," Condovian said confidently.

"Why not?" I asked.

"I can't believe you just asked my Dad to give you a vasectomy," Sledge said.

"Seriously, though, you're a Urologist, Condovian. It's what you do," I said.

"Listen, I'm not doing this," Condovian answered.

"Hear me out. I've researched this. It's as routine of a doctor's visit as it can possibly be. It's a pop-in pop-out type of deal. You could even do it while stoned. It's so easy!"

"Obviously I fucking know that, Beau. I give vasectomies for a living."

"Well...how about it then?" I asked.

"Condovian sat in silence. His eyes wandered around. He was thinking about it. His eyes moved toward the table and settled on the bag of weed," I told Arno.

"It's good stuff," I added.

"The 16 versus 1 game was about to end, when a commercial came on advertising the eight versus nine matchup, which was about to follow this very game. It was next. On top of that, it was the eighth seed, UNC - the University of North Carolina, versus the ninth seed, USC - the University of Southern California. Condovian cracked a smirk. It was my home state team versus his. It was fate."

"Fuck it. You've got UNC," Condovian said.

"Is there a point spread?" I questioned.

"Whoever wins, wins," Condovian answered.

"Alriiiiiiiiiiight let's do this," I said as I leaned over and shook Condovian's hand.

"Unreal," Sledge said.

"Sledge, not a word to your mother about this, or to anybody, ever," Condovian ordered.

"Obviously," Sledge responded. "But I get some of that bud if you win."

"Done," Condovian promised.

"Sledge, your Dad is the man," I said. "Now, let's roll another one for the game."

"This Condovian guy sounds like an asshole," Arno said.

"He's the man," I continued. "The bet was on."

"I remember that game well. It swayed a lot of bets on my end." Arno said.

"I don't remember the game well at all," I continued. "Just the ending. It turned out that the combination of weed, beer and a comfortable couch after a ridiculously long drive was too much for me to handle. My body shut down. While sitting upright, I drifted asleep. As a North Carolinian, I felt pretty good about letting my home state team decide the fate of any accidental children that I may or may not have had in the future. If UNC won, my vas would get severed - in a good way. If USC won, then not only would I have been out of weed, but my vas would've still been intact. That would have sucked. If USC won, I probably would've gotten someone pregnant within the week. When it rains, it pours."

"Did you sleep through the entire game?" Arno asked.

"Almost…almost," I continued. "I awoke to the loud sound of a buzzer. It startled me. I sat up, unsure of where I was or what was happening. I looked to my left and saw Condovian. I looked to my right and saw Sledge. They were both on the edge of their seats. I felt lost. I looked straight ahead and saw basketball."

"Sorry, Beau," Sledge said. "We had to switch it from the music to the game for the end of this thing."

"I couldn't find any words. I tried to focus on the screen enough to read the score. I could see both teams walking back onto the court from their benches. When my vision totally settled, the score read: 76 – 74, USC had the lead. There were 10 seconds remaining in the game. I looked over towards Condovian.

"What do ya' think, Beau?" Condovian said.

"I still couldn't seem to speak, so I grunted in acknowledgment," I told Arno.

"UNC's ball, down by two, 10 seconds to go. Vasectomies are on the line," Sledge continued. *"I bet I'm the first person in the history of the universe to say that line."*

"Alright, here we go boys," Condovian jumped in.

"A UNC player was about to pass the ball in from mid-court. The ref handed him the ball and blew his whistle. On the sound of the whistle, a million butterflies awoke in my stomached, and fluttered violently. He passed the ball inbounds, and the clock ticked to 9 seconds. Now, I was completely zoned into the game. UNC's point guard ran into the backcourt and caught the ball. The clock rolled to 8, and then 7. He dribbled into the frontcourt and stood, watching the clock tick down. It went to 6, and then 5. He looked confident. The clock seemed to move in slow motion. With 4 seconds to go, UNC's center ran above the three-point line to set a screen. The point guard faked as if he was going to run right, and then he went back to his left. The clock hit 3, and then 2. With one second left on the clock, he jumped from behind the three-point line and let the ball fly."

"Oh yeah, I definitely remember this game. That three pointer turned the game into a really nice pull for me. I think I cleared 500 large on that game alone," Arno said.

"I love the buzzer beater. It's one of my favorite moments in sports. It's up there with the walk-off homerun in baseball. It's much better than a game-winning field goal in football. I couldn't think of something more anti-climatic than a game-winning field goal. With buzzer-beaters, there's a total silence in the stadium for a brief moment. If the ball swishes through the net, the crowd erupts in unison, uncontrollably, waving their arms in the air, hugging strangers. What could be better?"

"I must admit," Arno continued. "I love it too."

SWISH!

"The ball dropped through the net. UNC won.

"I love it," Arno said. "Serves Condovian right."

"Right? I mean, how can you even blame me for being addicted to gambling when moments like that happened?" I asked.

"I can blame you because you still owe me 100 large," Arno said. "So, how'd the vasectomy go?"

"Not too shabby."

Chapter XXII

THE VASECTOMY

"The next day Condovian and I went to the hospital. It was supposed to be his day off, but he decided he wanted to pay up his end up of the bet as quickly as possible and be done with it."

"You should have taken notes from Condovian, Beau," Arno said.

"Maybe so, maybe not. Condovian will never get up by a massive amount, because he's scared to let it ride. I'm not."

"Clearly," Arno said. "But he'll also, most likely, never be tied up in someone's basement due to gambling debts."

"Touché," I continued. "When we got to the hospital, we didn't stop at a front desk or anything. We simply walked to a wing of the hospital, that seemed to be empty, and into one of the rooms."

"Alright, Beau. Get naked and put this gown on," Condovian said as he handed me the hospital gown."

"I changed and jumped up onto the chair. It was one of the chairs doctors use to examine pregnant women down under. There was a spot to rest my feet while I sat spread eagle. It was a great view for Condovian."

"Alright, Beau. The procedure that I'm about to perform is called a nonsurgical vasectomy. I only need to make a slight puncture wound to cut and tie your vas. After that, I'll repeat that procedure on the opposite side of your scrotum, and then we'll be all finished. You'll barely feel a thing"

"So, when I ejaculate, is anything going to come out?"

"Absolutely. It simply won't have the sperm necessary to impregnate a woman."

"What about my sex drive? As of now, I can get an erection-on-demand. I'd prefer to keep that trait intact."

"Your sex drive, along with any erection-on-demand abilities you may or may not have, will be unaffected," Condovian answered.

"Vasectomies are awesome," I declared.

"Dammit," Condovian Said.

"What's wrong?" I questioned frantically.

"Nothing, I just can't believe I'm doing this." Condovian answered.

"Maybe you should say, 'I can't believe I'm doing this' instead of 'Dammit' the next time you have a scalpel next to my manhood. I got nervous."

"UNC won because of the luckiest shot I've ever seen."

"It was clutch," I said. "Now, let's be careful down there."

"Lucky," Condovian responded.

"Regardless, we're here."

"Which is ridiculous...let's go double or nothing on the next game."

"Double or nothing?" I questioned. "I don't even know what double or nothing means in this scenario. A vasectomy reversal against two ounces of weed?"

"Well, the reversal isn't guaranteed to work. But I would like to try and acquire two ounces of weed."

"I think I'll stop while I'm ahead. Normally, I'd let it ride, but I can't imagine anything else I want at the moment. I don't want this vasectomy reversed, nor do I want to give up two ounces of weed."

"One of these days, you're going to get burnt, bad, in a bet. It's going to land you in some hot water, Beau."

"If Condovian could only see you now," Arno chimed in.

"What can I say? I should have knocked on some wood. Anyway, Condovian shook his head from side to side in disapproval. Having a pissed off urologist performing my vasectomy wasn't comforting," I told Arno.

"So, Beau, why get a vasectomy so young? You're only 25 right?" Condovian asked.

"Well, I guess it's because I felt like I had a potential $500,000 bill attached to my penis that could be delivered to me at any random moment," I told him.

"You can get a lot of tax benefits when you have children," Condovian said.

"Or you can get a Ferrari when you don't have children. Plus, I don't base any decisions on taxes. Taxes are going to suck no matter what, but at least they don't ever have a high-pitched cry."

"Did you have friends when you were really young, Beau?" Condovian asked.

"Of course I did! What kind of question is that?" I responded, slightly offended.

"So you liked kids when you were a kid?" Condovian questioned.

"Well, yeah, but, I was a kid too."

"Do any other age groups annoy you?" he asked.

"I wouldn't say that kids annoy me. I just don't want the responsibility of raising one. However, the thought of being extremely old definitely freaks me out. Old to the point where you just kind of sit there all day, waiting to die. I never want to be that old."

"So it's mainly children and old people your not fans of?"

"Don't make me sound like an asshole, Condovian. I like old people, I just feel sorry for them, and I don't want to be one of them. But yes, I'm not the biggest fan of children."

"I thought you were a free spirit liberal hippie, Beau."

"Kind of," I answered with a dash of confusion.

"You liberal hippies are all about equal rights for humans," Arno said.

"I know, and I'm all for that."

"Well, you need to change the way you look at children and old people then. They are humans. They should have every right that you have. Children should be able to have fun, regardless if that means a random 25 year-old guy gets annoyed. Kids are kids. They live to have fun. Don't be a party pooper. As for old people who are close to death, they deserve more respect than anybody for living as long as they have. They aren't gross. They are just dying. They should be sent off as comfortably as possible. You definitely shouldn't pity them. You should celebrate them and treat them like heroes."

"I searched for words, but came up empty. I had no rebuttal. Condovian was right. I don't know when I got it into my head that I didn't like kids, but I was wrong in doing so," I told Arno.

"Hey, Condovian?"

"Yes, Beau?"

"How far along into this surgery are we."

"Almost finished."

"Well I was just thinking about what you said, and I think, if we aren't too far along, maybe we should rethink this vasectomy thing. Maybe I do want a Beau Allen, Jr."

"We're too far along for that. Sorry, Beau."

"Oh," I said in a state of confusion.

"So you wanted to turn back at the last moment?" Arno asked.

"When reality sunk in, I did. I would never be able to have children. It's like I said, in retrospect, I would have loved for it to work with Isabella."

"Look on the bright side, Beau." Condovian continued. *"You said it yourself. There are some advantages to not having children. You'll be able to travel the world. You most likely won't have any financial problems, once you get a job. You and your future wife will probably stay together forever. Kids cause a lot of stress between husband and wife. Stress can eventually lead to a divorce. And if you ever really want kids, you can just adopt them. There are plenty of kids in need of a good home."*

"You're right, you're right. Or, I was right. I don't know. Fuck it - what's done is done," I said.

"That's the spirit, kind of," Condovian continued. "Aaaaaand we're finished!"

"Thanks, Condovian," I said.

"You're the proud new owner of a severed vas. Congratulations."

"Ha! Thanks Condovian."

"You're welcome. Now get out of here, go smoke weed with Sledge and do nothing for a few days," Condovian said.

"The exchange brightened my mood. I left thinking that I might get that Ferrari one day after all. I was safe and sterile with a new, brighter outlook on both children and old people," I said.

"Touching, Beau," Arno responded.

"So what do you think?"

"I don't know. I need to sleep on it," he continued. "I'll have your verdict tomorrow."

"Good call - it's always smart to sleep on it."

"I'll see you tomorrow," Arno said.

"Sweet dreams."

"Don't kiss my ass, Beau."

Chapter XXIII

JOHNNY'S GRANDMA

Saturday morning...

Beau's cell phone records had just been faxed to Detective Hunt. The last number to call Beau was registered to Johnny Santoro. Detective Hunt's heart sank. She knew Johnny was connected. However, as she scanned through the rest of the records, she noticed that the number Beau most frequently associated with didn't belong to Johnny – but to Liliana Santoro, also known as Johnny's Grandma. Her curiosity peaked. She left the police station and headed to Winnie's hotel. When she arrived, Winnie had just finished perfecting her hair and makeup for the day. She was ready to find Beau. After a quick stop for coffee, Winnie and Detective Hunt headed to Johnny's Grandma's to ask a few questions. When they arrived, they went over the game plan.

"Okay, Winnie," Detective Hunt continued. "This house belongs to a Liliana Santoro. Beau talks with someone at this house frequently."

"Liliana Santoro. Liliana Santoro," Winnie repeated to herself. "I don't believe Beau has ever mentioned a Liliana Santoro to me."

"Well, I ran a background check on her, Winnie. I've got some good news, and I've got some bad news.

"Start with the good, dear."

"The good news is that she's 99 years old with no prior arrests."

"Sounds like I can take her myself, sweetie. I'll be back in a few," Winnie said as she reached for her door handle.

"Hold on, Winnie," Detective Hunt said. When Winnie looked at her, she could see the genuine worry in her eyes. Now was not the time to inform her about Liliana Santoro's mafia connections. "Just let me do the talking, okay?"

"I will, sweetie," Winnie replied. "Anyway, she's 99. How threatening can she possibly be to my Beau? What was the bad news?"

"Just that I was going to do all the talking. I thought you might be disappointed about not being able to ask questions," Detective Hunt continued. "Ready?"

"I am. Let's do it," Winnie replied.

Winnie and Detective Hunt exited their car and walked to the front door of the house. Johnny's Grandma's Buick was the only car in the driveway. When they got to the door, they knocked. There was no answer. They knocked again, harder. This time, Liliana's voice sounded from inside.

"Just a sec!" Liliana yelled as loud as she could, which was still pretty quiet.

Winnie and Detective Hunt waited patiently for the door to open, which seemed to take a very long time.

"Do you think she's hiding something, dear? It seems to be taking her a while," Winnie asked Detective Hunt.

"I'm not sure, Winnie. She is 99 - it probably just takes her a little while to get to the door.

Just as Detective Hunt finished responding, the door opened, and in front of them stood Johnny's Grandma.

"Mrs. Santoro?" Detective Hunt asked.

"Yes," Johnny's Grandma said slowly and sweetly. "You can call me Lily."

"Okay, Lily. My name is Detective Hannah Hunt. This nice lady to my right is Paula Allen."

"You can call me Winnie," Winnie chimed in.

"May we come in for a moment?" Detective Hunt asked.

"Is there a problem?" Johnny's Grandma asked.

"No ma'am," Detective Hunt continued. "We just have a couple questions about a young man named Beau Allen."

"Beau Allen?" She asked.

"Yes ma'am. Do you know him?"

"It sounds familiar, but I can't put my thumb on it. Come on in."

"Can I offer either of you a chocolate chip cookie? They just came out of the oven."

"No thank you, Lily," Detective Hunt responded.

"Winnie, would you like one?"

"No thank you," Winnie continued. "But do you need any help with those?"

"Only with eating them. You're both missing out!" Johnny's Grandma said.

"So, Lily, you said that the name, Beau Allen, sounded familiar. Do you remember where you might have heard the name?"

"No, I don't. But then again, my memory isn't what it used to be. I do believe I've heard it before, though."

"The reason I ask, Lily, is because Beau is currently missing."

"Oh no! I'm sorry to hear that."

"He's my Grandson," Winnie informed her.

"You poor lady! I hope that they find him," Lily said.

"The reason we're telling you this, Lily, is because Beau frequently conversed with someone at this address before he went missing."

"Hmmm, that's strange. I know the name sounds familiar to me, but if I were dialing his number, I would surely remember."

"So, you didn't make the call to 917-555-4872?"

"No, I did not."

"Does anyone routinely use the phone other than you?"

"Well, sure!" Lily continued, "Family and friends visit me all the time. I'm a lucky woman!"

"Do you remember which family members or friends were at your residence on Tuesday, January 4th of this year?"

"Tuesday, January 4th?" she continued. "I'm afraid I don't. At my age, all of the days and dates seem to blend together. I lose track! What is today's date?"

"Today is Saturday, January 8th."

"I'm so sorry. I wish I could help, but I can't remember for the life of me who would have been here that long ago," Johnny's Grandma said.

"No problem, Lily." Detective Hunt continued, "If we have any more questions, would you mind if we stopped back by?"

"Not at all," she responded. "Anything I can do to help!"

"Thank you very much. We'll get out of your hair now!"

"Ok, then. Drive safely. Are you both sure you wouldn't like a cookie for the road? They're my specialty!"

"Thank you, but no thank you," Detective Hunt said.

"I'll pass as well, dear," Winnie said.

"Good luck, Winnie. I hope you find your grandson."

"Thank you, Lily."

Winnie and Detective Hunt left Johnny's Grandma's house, having come so close, yet so far, to finding Beau. Lily Santoro may have had a weak memory, but Winnie was sharp as a tack, and her gut told her that they were on to something. When they returned to the car, Winnie gave her observations.

"I've got a funny feeling about this place, sweetie," Winnie continued. "Beau has been here before. Lily Santoro may be 99 years old, but she's sharper than she just led us to think. I think she knows where my Beau is. We should search this house, dear," Winnie continued. "Right now!"

"We'll need to get a warrant to do that," Detective Hunt continued. "And we need more evidence. In the meantime, let's head to Chris Zuber's residence. It was another person who frequently called Beau. We'll interview him and see where it leads."

"OK, sweetie. I feel like we're close. We're going to save my Beau!"

Chapter XXIII

JUDGMENT DAY

It seemed as if Arno was only gone for an hour or two before the front door opened and slammed again. I, obviously, had not slept a wink. My stomach had been in knots. I had not been able to think of anything other than dying. Up until this point, despite being tied up in this basement, I had kept a weird confidence that I would survive. I felt that Arno had not only begun to like me, but he had begun to respect me as well.

Today was different. I was scared. I didn't want to be remembered the way my family and friends would remember me if I disappeared for good. I was ashamed at how I had accomplished nothing in my life. I was embarrassed of how many mistakes I had made. I hated how many regrets I held. I wanted to turn back the clock and do it all over again.

Unfortunately, life doesn't give any do-overs - but I still wanted to redeem myself. I did not want to die. I wanted the chance to actually make something of myself.

BAM! The lights flicked on. It was Arno, and it was judgment day. Arno slowly walked down the steps. It felt like one of those "I have bad news" walks that waiters and waitresses do after they accidentally accept an order for an item that is out of stock. I couldn't handle the suspense any longer.

"You're going to kill me, aren't you?" I asked.

Arno took a deep breath as he arrived at the bottom of the staircase. It was definitely one of those deep breaths people take before delivering bad news. Fuck. "Beau," he began. "To tell you the truth, I still haven't decided. I don't know why this has been such a tough decision for me. Normally, I can make the decision on whether or not to kill someone in an instant, and then never think about it again. For some reason, with you, I just can't make up my mind. I don't really want to kill you, but at the same time, I feel slightly obligated to. You did fuck me out of $100,000 after all. And it's not smart to leave any type of witnesses to any crime."

"I'll figure out a way to pay you back. I'll take out a loan."

"Yeah, but then we have to go through that whole weekly collection process. You might not be able to pay one week, and then we'd be right back in the same boat we're in right now. Or, you might run. If you ran, then we'd end up back in the torture boat, but there would be no more stories. We'd simply torture you in all the ways you don't want, and then kill you. It's such a tiring process, you know? I'd be willing to just give you the bullet to the head today if you wanted. It would be quick and easy for you. You wouldn't feel a thing. It's almost like I would be doing you a favor, and we could all move on," Arno said as he pulled his gun out of his waistline.

"I wouldn't move on! And as much I appreciate the offer of a quick bullet to the head, because I think it would be a great way to go, I have to tell you Arno, I don't want to die. I want to live."

"Of course you do. Who doesn't?"

"Well, let me live then, dammit!"

"It's not that easy, Beau."

"Sure it is. You're the boss. Just say I can live and I'll live."

"No," he said.

"Goddammit."

"Easy, Beau. Easy."

"Excuse me, Arno. This is just a very frustrating ordeal for me, to say the least. Where's Johnny at?"

"He dropped me off. He has something he needs to take care of," Arno continued. "So is this the first time you've had a near-death experience?"

"No, but the first time I was really fucked up, so I wasn't able to comprehend that situation as well as this one. I've had nothing to do but think about this situation for however fucking long I've been down in this basement. What day is it anyway?"

"It's Saturday morning."

"Fuck. I've only been here for 5 days! I thought it had been weeks."

"Yep...now you see why I need to go ahead and make a decision on this thing. Pretty soon Johnny's Grandma will be able to charge you rent, and rightfully so!"

"This thing? Is that a joke? This thing is my life, Arno!"

"Excuse me, Beau. I thought you were all about humor," he responded.

"I am, but I didn't like that joke. It was a terrible joke."

"It wasn't that bad," Arno said as he stretched and yawned.

"Prison has to be better than this," I remarked.

"Yeah, it probably is," Arno continued. "Are you scared of the slammer?"

"Of course. Although, I don't think it would be that terrible if I was the prisoner who ran the show. I'd be okay with being the top dog. It would be slightly depressing, but doable."

"Interesting," Arno said.

"Have you ever done time?" I asked.

"Nothing major. A year here and there when I was younger for theft, but I was always the guy who ran the show inside."

"Nice."

"It still sucks, but it makes it much more tolerable, that's for sure," he responded.

KNOCK, KNOCK, KNOCK!

"What the fuck was that?" Arno said as he grabbed his gun.

"Sounded like someone knocking on the front door upstairs." I said.

"Shut the fuck up, Beau. Not another fucking word," he said as he pointed the gun in my face.

A few seconds went by, and then another *KNOCK, KNOCK, KNOCK!* It was louder this time that it was the last."

"Complete fucking silence!" Arno whispered.

I heard Johnny's Grandma's muffled voice, a door open and shut - followed by the sound of footsteps. There were multiple people walking around. I was used to this sound, but Arno was clearly agitated. We sat in total silence for about five minutes. When the front door opened and shut once more, we waited for another five minutes in total silence. Arno put his gun back on the table.

"Stay here," he demanded, as he slowly stood up and crept up the stairs.

This was my chance! He left his fucking *gun* down here! When Arno got to the top of the steps, he cracked the basement door open and spied through. After a few moments, he opened the door all the way, left the basement and shut the door behind him. I began to wiggle as violently as possible. I was able to get my feet on the ground and pushed myself from side to side. After a few strong sways, the chair tipped over, and I fell to the ground with it. When I hit the ground, I heard a large *CRACK!* The right armrest had snapped! I was able to slip my arm through. I grabbed the poorly tied knot on my left and pulled the rope, rendering my left hand free as well.

BAM!

The basement door swung open. I grabbed the poorly tied knots around my feet, yanked them and slipped my feet out.

"What the fuck, Beau!" Arno yelled as he sprinted down the stairs.

I stood up just in time and dove for the gun at the same time as Arno. We crashed into the table, sending the gun flying across the room. Arno's fist smashed across my face. I threw my left fist into his gut and followed with my right fist into his face. He stumbled back. I continued with another left-right combo, and then hit him with a third. My adrenaline was pumping. I felt like I had the strength of a normal sized man. Arno fell backwards to the ground. Stupidly, I ran for the stairs, instead of the gun. I was almost to the top when I felt myself being yanked through the air.

BAM!

I slammed into the bottom of the stairs and rolled onto the basement floor.

"You are one stupid motherfucker, Beau. I was literally about to decide to let you live," Arno said, panting heavily as he kicked me in the ribs.

"I had to, Arno," I continued, wincing in pain. "You left me an opening. You would've done the same."

BAM!

His right fist smashed into my nose.

"And that's for punching me in the face, you asshole. I'm going to have a black eye! Now stay right fucking there!"

"I could've grabbed the gun and shot you, but I didn't," I said.

"You should have."

"I just wanted to get away. I didn't want to kill you. I thought we were bros."

"Fuck you, Beau."

Arno walked backwards to the corner of the basement, and grabbed another chair. He threw the chair in my direction.

"Pick it up!"

I picked it up.

"Now sit the fuck down!"

I sat down. Arno pulled out his cellphone and dialed a number.

"Johnny!" He yelled. "Grab the PeNabs and get over to your Grandma's house NOW! Let's have some fun!"

Fuck.

Chapter XXIV

ZUBER

Saturday afternoon...

Much like Beau, Zuber lived in an extremely small studio apartment where the bed folds out of the wall. The moment that Winnie and Detective Hunt arrived at his front door, they could smell marijuana.

KNOCK, KNOCK, KNOCK!

"Who is it?" Zuber yelled.

"Detective Hannah Hunt of the NYPD, and Pau---Winnie. We'd like to have a word!"

Zuber obliged. The door opened about an inch before the chain lock prevented it from opening any further.

"What's this about?" Zuber questioned.

"I can assure you it has nothing to do with the strong smell of marijuana coming from your apartment," Detective Hunt responded.

Zuber's face turned as red as his eyes.

"It's about a missing person, Beau Allen," she continued.

"Beau is missing?"

"For almost a week now."

"Oh my God, no way!"

"May we come in?"

"Absolutely, come on in."

The door shut, and the sound of the chain sliding out of its lock followed. When the door opened, there stood Zuber. He was about 5'9", had fair skin, dark brown hair, a constant 5 o'clock shadow, and glasses.

"Thank you," Detective Hunt said. "This is Winnie, Beau's Grandma."

"No way!" Zuber said. "I hate that we have to meet under these circumstances, but Beau talks about you all the time!"

"Nice to meet you, Sweetie," Winnie said as she gave Zuber a hug.

"Would either of you like something to drink? I have water and beer."

"No thank you," they replied.

"So, Zuber," Detective Hunt began. "When was the last time you saw Beau?"

"I saw Beau last Sunday."

"Where did you see him?

"Santoros' Sports bar in Manhattan. We watched the Falcons game together."

"Did Beau seem to be acting normal to you?" Detective Hunt questioned.

"Absolutely. Beau was a couple of beers deep by the time I arrived, and was being his usual, social self."

"Do you know if Beau had any enemies, or people he had been in recent arguments with?"

"No ma'am," Zuber responded.

"None at all?"

"Well…"

There was a name at the top of his mind, but he absolutely did not want to say it. Detective Hunt picked up on his hesitation.

"Beau's been missing for nearly a week, Zuber. His life may be in extreme danger at this point. ANY information you can give us could potentially save his life."

"Okay," Zuber said uncomfortably. "There's a name that you should look into, but I absolutely do not want my name mixed up in ANY of this. I will not testify under any circumstance. I just know one person that Beau may have been in a bit of debt with."

"What's the name?"

"I'm serious. This can't get back to me at all."

"It won't."

"Johnny Santoro."

Winnie and Detective Hunt exchanged looks. Now, they were on to something.

"He owns Santoro's Sports Bar in Manhattan…and he's…well, he's…"

"He's what?" Detective Hunt asked.

"*Connected,*" Zuber whispered.

"Thank you, Zuber. You've been a tremendous help. We'll be back if we have any more questions," Detective Hunt said as she urgently stood up. "Winnie, let's go."

"Thank you, sweetie," Winnie said, as she hugged Zuber and planted a big kiss on his cheek. As with all Winnie kisses, it left the outline of her red lipstick on his cheek.

Winnie and Detective Hunt left Zuber's apartment and headed for Santoro's Sports Bar. However, when they arrived, they found no sign of Johnny.

"It's getting a bit late, Winnie," Detective Hunt began. "I'm going to drop you off at the hotel and make some calls to see if I can figure out any of Johnny's other hangouts. Try to get some sleep, and I will pick you up first thing in the morning."

"I can help you do that, sweetie."

"You need to get some rest."

Reluctantly, Winnie responded, "Okay, dear. But come bright at early. I'm just worried sick now."

"I will, Winnie. I'll be here at 7:30 on the dot."

"Okay, sweetie."

Chapter XXV

THE OLD SEX GAG - PART THREE

The smirk on Johnny's face as he trotted down the basement steps was infuriating. I wanted to smash it. But, seeing as how Arno had tied my arms and legs to the chair with knots that would make an Eagle Scout proud, that didn't seem to be an option. To make matters worse, Johnny had that old sex gag in his hand again. Dammit. I decided then and there, if they want me quiet, I'm not going to give them the pleasure of another word. Fuck them, and fuck that sex gag. Gross.

The PeNabs trotted down after Johnny. They were both carrying small duffle bags over their shoulders. It was now a party. When they saw Arno's bruised and slightly bloodied face, they were ready to make my worst nightmares come true.

"What happened to your face, boss?" Johnny questioned.

"This cocksucker punched me."

"He punched you?"

"A few times," Arno responded.

"You really are a dumb motherfucker, Beau. You don't hit made guys. You definitely don't hit the fucking boss."

I said nothing. I simply stared at Johnny. I hoped that he could see the hatred in my eyes. I really don't even mind Arno and the PeNabs. Arno was actually a pretty cool dude and the PeNabs seemed happy. It's hard to hate happy people. Johnny was the buzz kill.

"I asked you a question!" Johnny yelled before he punched me in the face. "That felt good. Anyway, how'd he get free to punch you in the face, boss?"

"Bad knots. We had a scuffle. I won, obviously."

"So I guess you don't mind if I punch him in the face again?"

"Not at all," Arno said.

BAM! His fist smashed across my right eye for the second time. That one stung.

"I don't know what it is about your face that's so much fun to hit, Beau, but I gotta' tell ya', it's a damn good time."

I stayed silent.

"Nothing to say about that, Beau?" Johnny asked. "Fine, if you don't want to talk, we'll just put the old sex gag back in your mouth."

He went to strap the gag around my head. I twisted and turned until the PeNabs helped him hold my head straight. They got the gag in.

"Okay, what's first, boys?" Arno asked.

"Give me the rope, PeNab," Johnny said.

One of the PeNabs handed Johnny a decent amount of rope.

"Let's start with hanging him upside down and letting the blood rush to his head for a while," Johnny suggested.

"That's not very torturous," Arno said.

"No, it's not," Johnny continued. "But it's what Beau's afraid of."

The PeNabs untied my feet from the chair and retied them together with the new rope while leaving a long section of extra rope. Next, they untied my hands and retied them together in handcuff form behind my back.

"Lay down," Johnny demanded.

One of the PeNabs took the extra rope and threw it over a rafter from the ceiling.

"PeNab, you pick him, feet first, up for a minute. PeNab, you pull the rope."

When they did this, I was lifted into the air. Johnny grabbed the rope, tied it into a knot, and then walked in front of me. I was suspended in the air, swinging like a pendulum.

"Perfect," Johnny said. "He's like my own personal punching bag."

He bashed his left fist, then his right, then left, then right, into my ribcage. I could only grunt and fight to breathe through my nose.

"Arno, you want to give him a few punches. It's fun…"

Arno looked into my eyes before replying, "Why not?" He stood up and copied Johnny, with fist after fist crashing into my stomach and rib cage. His punches hurt worse than Johnny's, but what else would you expect from the boss?

"I must admit. That did feel pretty good. It's kind of a rush, Beau," Arno said while panting. "What's next?"

"I think we should let him hang for a bit and get some more blood in his head."

I hated that idea. My head was already starting to throb in pain. I felt like I was close to passing out and it had only been a few moments. I kept telling myself to do was breathe, slowly but surely, through my nose.

"After that, we've got options," Johnny continued. "Let's see...if I'm remembering correctly, he didn't want to be burned or shot in a non-lethal location. Also, he hates snakes and spiders. Maybe we can put a few spiders on him and light him on fire - while shooting him in the arms and legs?

"I like the thought, but then this thing would be over rather quickly. And fuck spiders. Let's go step by step. I want Beau to be able to appreciate each torture method. PeNab, you have a lighter?" Arno asked.

PeNab pulled a lighter from his pocket and handed it to Arno.

"Perfect. Here ya' go, Johnny. Give him a few good burns. Don't light him all the way on fire though."

"It would be an honor boss," Johnny said, smiling. "Now, where to start, where to start?"

"Do his hands first," Arno said. "Any motherfucker who lays their hands on me deserves to have them burnt."

"Consider it done, boss man," Johnny said. "PeNab, grab his arms and make sure he doesn't squirm."

The PeNabs both grabbed my arms. Each one of them was twice as strong as I was on their own, but with both of them, there was absolutely no chance that I would be able to budge an inch. Johnny knelt down in front of me. I tried to watch him, but it hurt my eyes to look up while hanging upside down, so I just closed them. There was nothing I could do about it anyway, so fuck it.

"Isn't this fun, boss?" Johnny asked.

CLICK!

I heard the lighter flick, and felt the warmth near my hands. That warmth quickly turned into excruciating pain. I screamed into the gag as loud as I could. I twisted and turned with all my might. I must have found a strength I had not discovered until that moment, because not even both PeNabs could hold me still. Johnny laughed an awful laugh. I never thought that I would be capable of murdering someone. Having said that, if I had a gun at that moment, I would have blasted Johnny away, no questions asked. Then, I'd leave the basement while pointing the gun at Arno and the PeNabs. They still don't deserve to die in my book, at least not yet. Johnny is the only one getting a sick and twisted pleasure out of this.

"Where next, boss?" Johnny asked.

"Hmmm," Arno pondered. "Do the bottoms of his feet. That way he won't try to run again."

"You've got it. PeNabs, grab his legs. Hold him tighter this time too. We need to get a better burn on his feet than on his hands."

They grabbed my legs, and held on for what would most certainly be a ride. Johnny walked to the corner of the basement and grabbed another chair. He set it next to me and then climbed on top of it so that he could reach my feet.

CLICK!

The warmth returned over the bottoms of both of my feet. That warmth, once again, quickly turned into excruciating pain that sent me screaming, twisting and turning for relief. This time, however, I got a bit of relief. The PeNabs were unable to hold me still. I swung into Johnny's chair, and sent him crashing to the ground. My screams turned to laughs. Johnny did not appreciate it.

"Fuck you, Beau!" he yelled before punching my directly in the testicles. It was worse than the burns. I squealed in pain. "Not laughing now, are you? I didn't think so!"

I could hear Arno chuckling a bit on the side. I liked to think that he was chuckling at Johnny falling off of his chair, and not at the punch to my testicles.

"What now, boss?" Johnny asked.

"I'm not sure, Johnny," Arno began. "I mean, as much fun as this would normally be for me, I'm starting to feel bad about it for some reason. I've gotten to know Beau decently well over the past few days, and I kind of like the guy. I'm starting to think that I may have overreacted a bit from his attempted escape. JUST A BIT, though! Now, I'm thinking we should just end it."

"So soon?" Johnny questioned.

Arno ignored the question. "PeNab, you have your silenced pistol on you?" A PeNab pulled out the gun from his duffle bag. PeNab, you have the plastic and the bleach?" The other PeNab pulled out the plastic and the bleach.

I don't know if it was because I had been hanging upside down for too long, or because the threats were getting serious, but I got light-headed.

"Wait a second, boss." Johnny said. "Let's at least pop him in the arm a couple times, first. I feel like Beau NEEDS to experience that before checking out of this world."

Arno stared at him, seemingly trying to decide whether to shoot me in the arms or the head. "Fuck it, give him a couple of pops in the arms first," he said as he handed the silenced gun to Johnny. Johnny didn't hesitate.

POP! POP!

The first bullet went into my left bicep, and the second into my right bicep. It felt as if someone had drilled holes into both arms and dumped boiling hot water inside. It was unbearable. I squirmed and squirmed while screaming as loud as I could into the gag. Johnny was right. This was my worst nightmare. Or so I thought, until I heard Arno say, "Okay, I've seen enough. Let's end it."

I stopped squirming and attempted to yell, "WAIT!" over and over again.

"Any last words, Beau?" Johnny asked rhetorically while chuckling. He lifted the gun and pointed it at my head.

"WAIT!" Arno yelled. "I'm actually somewhat interested in his last words. PeNab, take the gag out of his mouth. I want to hear what he has to say. Sure, he's done some absurdly stupid shit that he should not have done, but I've grown to respect him a little bit. He's no rat...just a shitty gambler."

I knew it. He did respect me a bit. PeNab unhooked the gag from my mouth.

"Goddamn getting shot hurts!"

"So, Beau, any last words?" Arno asked.

"Ahhhhhhhh!" I yelled. My arms were absolutely throbbing in pain.

"Stop being a little bitch, Beau. Do you have any last words?" Johnny asked.

"Yeah...give me a second, though. I forgot about the last words. I want them to be good," I pleaded.

"Beau," Arno continued. "You've seriously been sitting down here for almost a week with your death looming, and you haven't thought about your last words?"

"You're right, you're right," I continued. "I probably should have thought about the last words, but I was holding out hope, ya' know? Are y'all going to make sure my last words are heard?"

"Is that a serious question?" Arno asked.

"Yes..."

"Beau, we're about to put you six feet deep. No one is even going to know you're dead. They'll probably suspect it after no one hears from you, but they'll never find a body. They'll never know for sure. Jimmy fucking Hoffa, baby! We're not going to kill you and then go public with it. Hey everyone, we just murdered Beau, but here were his last words - please don't press any charges. Does that make a hell of a lot of sense to you?" Arno answered.

"Well, I guess you have a point. But that also completely changes everything then, doesn't it?" I continued. "No one but you, Johnny and the PeNabs will know what I said, and I'm not sure if y'all deserve that pleasure or not."

"Regardless what you think, as of now those were your last words, so we've got that pleasure anyway."

"Dammit, I guess you've got another point," I continued. "Can you at least make an awesome speech before doing this thing? Something that makes my whole life make sense before I go?"

"A speech?" he asked.

"Yeah. All the legendary mob bosses are doing it. You should *always* give a reason and a badass speech to your victims."

Arno stayed silent for a moment. He looked distraught.

"What's wrong, Arno?" I asked.

"Nothings wrong, dammit. I'm just thinking about a speech now."

"Well, while you're waiting, I think I've got a few last words for you."

"Let's hear them," Arno said.

"First of all, you violated the mustache code. Anyone with a bold mustache, such as yours, or the one I previously owned, should have respect for it, and never wish harm on it. I wouldn't ever shave your mustache. Do you know why?" I asked.

"Unbelievable," Arno responded. "Why, Beau?"

"Because I respect the mustache, and you should, too. I think it's despicable that you don't. You said I didn't deserve a mustache because I wasn't able to pay my debts? I say you don't deserve a mustaches because you don't know dick about mustaches...or bone-chilling speeches for that matter," I ranted. "Just go ahead and pull the trigger. Get this moment over with. You need to put it behind you as soon as possible. Your legacy will say that you were a feared and ruthless boss. However, you were a feared and ruthless boss who never had the ability to make that last bone-chilling speech when it counted most. It's a shame. You were so close to being great. A legend."

Arno shook his head from side to side and laughed. "All the way until the very end, Beau. You're ridiculous. I don't think I'll ever be able to forget this whole ordeal."

"You've still got a chance to make it right," I said.

"How so?" Arno continued. "By letting you go?"

"Well, that would be awesome, but that's not what I was going to say."

"How then?"

"There's one way to die, where if I absolutely have to die, would be a fitting exit for me. Also, it would give you time to shave my face into a mustache, which would effectively prove your respect for lip sweaters at the same time."

"The Viking funeral?" he asked.

"Well - that would be fitting. However, I was thinking more along the lines of overdosing."

"You want to overdose?"

"On molly. Your hands would be clean. Technically, you wouldn't have been the one to kill me. None of you would. Most importantly – there would be no mess to clean up. Unless it's true about shitting yourself when you die. I'll try not to, though..."

"Interesting," Arno said. "Why Molly?"

"Because it's awesome."

"Johnny, you ever do any of this Molly?" Arno asked.

"Absolutely not, boss. I'm no junkie."

"None of you have ever tried it?" I asked in disbelief. They all shook their heads no.

"You guys need to live a little. All we need is some girls, great music, beers, maybe a disco ball and a fog machine. Send me out in style!"

"This is ridiculous, boss. Let's just shoot him and be done with it."

"Hmmm," Arno pondered. "No, no, I think I'll allow it. You know where to get some of this stuff, Johnny?"

"I'm sure it wouldn't be a problem, boss. I can have the stuff and the girls waiting for me in the bar in an hour."

"Make it happen then. In the meantime, call Dr. Gray. Tell him to bring his medical kit to your grandma's. Cut Beau down, tie him back up in the chair, with good, solid knots, and then go get the goods," Arno ordered.

"And the shave?" I asked. "I'd like to die with my mustache – even if it is an incredibly weak one right now."

"'I'll take care of it, Beau," Arno said. "Johnny – make the calls. Let's get this show on the road."

Johnny looked frustrated, but he obliged. They cut me down and tied me back into the chair. It felt like home - especially after Johnny and the PeNabs left.

"Thanks, Arno," I said.

"You're welcome, but we're still going to stuff enough molly down your throat to kill you."

"Fair enough."

Shortly after, Dr. Gray arrived to get the bullets out of my arms. More importantly, he brought one last anesthesia shot with him. Clutch. I was looking forward to that shot. There's nothing like getting a little rest before the big sleep.

Chapter XXVII

BEAU ALLEN WAS A LITTLE BITCH

A priest stood in front of a small group of people at a cemetery. The group consisted of my mother and father, my sisters, Sledge and Condovian, Hal Simmons (who was asleep in his chair, most likely drunk), Zuber, Hallman, Mac, Chuck, Kimmy, Ashley, Molly, Dr. Robinson, Arno and the boys, Winnie and Detective Hannah Hunt, and last but not the youngest...Johnny's Grandma.

"Ladies and gentlemen," the priest began. "We're gathered here today to put Beau's body in the ground. He was a nice enough dude, but as a priest – I'm obligated to say the truth. Beau Allen was a little bitch. He let these guys over here torture him without doing a thing about it," he said as he pointed at Arno and the boys. "So, that's really all I've got. Mrs. Allen, Mr. Allen, do either of you have anything you want to add to that?"

My mother and father stood up and walked to the front of the group.

"Beau was always a little different," she said. "He was pretty hard to describe. I'm having trouble finding the right words."

My father leaned over and whispered into her ear.

"You're right," she said to him. "I guess the term 'little bitch' really does hit the nail on the head. I just hope that none of you think less of me for giving birth to such a

little bitch. If it's anyone's fault, it's my husband's fault. He's always had erectile dysfunction and a low sperm count."

My father stepped forward, "I just want to say that I'm sorry to everyone gathered here today for exposing your lives Beau. Any of my daughters would have found a way to survive Arno's torture sessions. Beau, however, most likely got comfortable and lazy down in Johnny's Grandma's basement, and just decided to sit there until he died. Also – I recently switched to boxers, so the low sperm count should be improving. The other thing isn't true. I promise I'm not like Beau. He wanted to be neutered - or something like that."

"I just want to say," Johnny interrupted as he stood up, "That this is my type of funeral. I tried telling Arno for the longest time. He kept getting on my case about giving Beau such a hard time in the basement. But I just kept telling him. I said, 'Boss man, this guy is a little bitch. You just gotta' trust me. I tend to call it like it is, just like you good people are doing here today. You're all welcome at Santoro's Sports Bar anytime. First round on the house.'"

"That's right," Arno said. "He did tell me over and over again. I'm sorry to everyone here. We could've been done with this whole thing a week ago. That's my bad, but what can I say? I wanted to hear Beau's tale so I could make sure that my own children never turned out to be like him. Can you blame me?"

"No, we can't, Arno," the priest chimed back in. "You're a good man. Would anyone else like to say anything?"

"I would," Dr. Robinson began. "Let me just start by saying that Beau was an interesting man. I once had a talk with Beau in my office. Afterwards, I recommended

that he get a vasectomy. I'm sure many of you were slightly confused by it at the time. Some of you may have even thought that I was insane. You may have hated me. But now, I think you all realize that I was right. I was just doing my civic duty. I was trying to prevent a little bitch from reproducing. So, I'll close by saying that I told you so."

"Let me interrupt for a moment, Doc," Arno said. "I'll be the first one to admit I was wrong about you. When Beau told me about you recommending a vasectomy, I couldn't imagine what type of therapist would do such a thing. Hindsight is 20-20, though, and now I just think we should all, as a group, say 'thank you' to this American Hero. Thank you, Dr. Robinson."

"Thank you, Dr. Robinson," the group said in unison.

"You're welcome, everybody," she responded.

"Sledge...Condovian...anything you want to add?" The priest asked.

"I'm good," Sledge said.

"I'll say something," Condovian said. "I appreciate that everyone thanked Dr. Robinson for the fantastic advice she gave to Beau, which did help rid the world of future little bitches. BUT, can we all thank me as well? I mean, after all, I am the one who went near that little bitch's scrotum and sliced his vas. Dr. Robinson might have been the brains of the operation, but I was the executioner."

"Touché," the priest said. "Everybody, let's give it up for Condovian. Let's say 'Thank you' and give him a little round of applause."

"Thank you, Condovian," The group said, this time while standing up and clapping.

"You're welcome, everybody. You're welcome."

"Hal?" The priest questioned. "Any words?"

Hal snored.

"I think he's shit-faced, father," Arno said. "He might've even pissed himself."

"Perfect, we'll all get out of here that much faster. I think we can assume that Hal would've agreed with us, right?"

The entire group nodded in approval.

"Hallman...any words?"

"Beau drank slowly and his jaw broke easily. What could I possibly have to say?"

"Alright then. How about you, Molly? After all...you did do some naughty things with that little bitch."

Molly's face turned red as she covered her face with her hands. Ashley and Kimmy spoke up for her, "She's embarrassed enough, father."

"Well I don't blame her," the priest continued. "Molly, say ten Hail Mary's and God might forgive you."

"Consider it done, father," Molly said.

"Zuber, how about you? You were pretty good friends with Beau, right?" The priest asked.

"I was father. Am I ashamed about it? No. Like "Amazing Grace" says... "I once was blind, but now I see." It won't happen again, father. I promise."

"You need to say ten Hail Mary's and five Our Father's. Peace be with you."

"I'm not Catholic, father," Zuber said.

"Do it anyway," the priest continued. "Now, let's put this little bitch on ice and go grab some lunch. Who's with me?"

The crowded cheered and began to stand.

"WAIT!" Winnie shouted. "Everyone, sit down. I have something to say."

"I'm not so sure about that, Winnie." The priest said.

"And why the hell not, father?"

"Well, to be perfectly honest, if you and Detective Hunt hadn't gone on your little scavenger Hunt, Arno and the Boys would have been able to do what they do best and make Beau simply...disappear...like Jimmy Hoffa. None of us would have ever been able to know with absolute certainty that Beau was, in fact, dead. We never would have had to have this funeral. We would have beat the lunch crowds that we're inevitably going to hit now, especially after a few more words.

"Sit down, father," Winnie demanded.

"Yes, ma'am," the priest said as he quickly sat down. Winnie stood and walked to the front.

"Now...I know that everyone thinks poorly of my Beau. Sure, he might have messed up a few time. Hell, I've even thought to myself once or twice that Beau just wasn't that great. But - that doesn't change one important thing."

"What's that, Winnie?" The priest asked impatiently, pointing to his watch.

"Beau was our little bitch. He was our little bitch. I don't know about you all, but I'm sad that he's gone. I loved my little bitch. I loved my Beau, and I want him back."

The group fell silent. It almost sounded as if someone let out a slight whimper. However, whoever whimpered did so quickly hid it. They didn't want to be caught crying over a little bitch.

"Winnie's right," Arno said as he stood and walked towards the casket. When he reached the casket, he grabbed the lid, opened it and spoke directly to Beau's corpse. "BEAU! Why'd you have to be such a little bitch? BEAU! BEAU! BEAU!"

"BEAU!" Arno yelled. I opened my eyes. Music was blaring. The basement's lights were dimmed. Arno was holding a mirror in front of my face. "Check it out. I've got your mustache looking sharp for your going away party. Not bad, eh?" He twisted the mirror slightly to show that both sides were even. "Johnny will be back with the PeNabs, molly and girls shortly. Are you ready?"

Today was the day I was going to die. I knew it.

"This mustache could really use two more weeks to reach its full potential."

"Nice try, Beau," Arno replied.

"What day is it?"

"Bright and early on a Sunday morning," Arno said.

"We're going to have the molly party first thing in the morning?" I asked.

"If I'm going to get fucked up, I need to do it early. Most of my business happens at night. I need to be sharp by then. I figure if we start early, I can probably get a powernap in mid-afternoon," he said.

"I guess it doesn't really matter what time it is anyways," I continued. "You know, I never really saw myself dying on a Sunday. I always thought that I'd die on a Friday or Saturday, maybe a Wednesday. But not Sunday."

"Why not Sunday?"

"I don't know, I'm normally just sitting on the couch on Sunday."

"It will probably be more like 10 or 11ish on a Sunday."

"What time is it now?"

"Almost 8 a.m. Johnny should be back any minute."

"Sunday at 10 or 11 a.m. Interesting."

"Cheer up, Beau. You're going to go out with a nice buzz."

"I doubt that. OD'ing doesn't sound pleasant at all. I'll be freaking out in my mind and I'll die in a state of utter confusion. I just said that to buy more time. I'll probably shit myself as soon as I die, too, so have fun with that."

"You better not shit yourself."

"I gotta' tell you, that's what I'm the most nervous about. I don't want to shit myself," I continued. "Just make me one promise."

"What's that?" Arno asked.

"If I do poop - make Johnny clean it up."

"Done."

Chapter XXVIII

LITTLE WHITE LIES

Sunday Morning...

Staying true to her word, Detective Hunt arrived at the hotel to pick Winnie up at 7:30 a.m. sharp. There was an uneasiness in the air. They both sensed the pressure was on.

"Good morning, Winnie."

"Good morning, sweetie," Winnie continued. "Where are we heading today?"

"We're going back to Lily Santoro's house in New Jersey. I think your hunch about her was right. Let's see if we can get her to slip and reveal something."

"I think that's a terrific idea, dear. Something just didn't feel quite right about her."

They headed for New Jersey. When they arrived at Liliana Santoro's just after 8 a.m., they saw Liliana sitting on the front porch, enjoying a cup of coffee. Winnie and Detective Hunt exited the car and approached.

"Good morning, Lily," Detective Hunt said as she walked up the steps of the front porch. "Do you remember me from yesterday morning?"

"I do," Lily said. "But I'm afraid I've forgotten your names."

"I'm Detective Hannah Hunt, and this is Winnie."

"That's right. I'm so forgetful these days. Did you have any luck finding that poor boy?"

"I'm afraid that's why we're back this morning," Detective Hunt said.

"Would either of you two ladies like a cup of coffee?" Lily offered.

"No, thank you," Winnie and Detective Hunt replied simultaneously.

"Okay, then. Please, have a seat."

They sat in the rocking chairs next to Lily's.

"Lily," Detective Hunt began. "Have you seen your grandson, Johnny, recently?"

"Of course. He visits me every day. He was here with his friends very early this morning. It must have been just before 5 a.m. or so. They were getting some party ideas for my 100th birthday party. I'm turning 100 years old in a couple days!"

"Well happy early birthday, Lily."

"Happy birthday, dear."

"Thank you both."

"Did Johnny say where he might be today? We have a couple questions that we would love to ask him."

"He didn't. He just came in, asked about my favorite flowers and decorations and then left."

"Did you recognize the friends he had with him?"

"I did. They're identical twins. I can't remember their names, though."

"Would you recognize most of Johnny's friends?" Winnie asked.

"I believe I would. I'm terrible with names, nowadays, but I can normally remember a face."

Winnie pulled out a photo of Beau.

"Do you remember this man?"

"I do! He's a funny young man. He always loved my cookies. He used to watch football over here with my Johnny, and he'd eat nearly the entire tray of cookies! They're good friends."

"This is Beau Allen. He's one who's missing."

"Oh no! I hate to hear that. I always liked that young man a lot."

"Do you know if Johnny has a certain spot that he likes to hangout at most days, or somewhere he regularly attends for lunch? We believe he may be able to help us find Beau," Detective Hunt asked.

"I'm sorry, I don't. I don't get out of the house very often. Johnny normally comes over here to visit me."

Winnie and Detective Hunt exchanged disappointed looks.

"Well if you he comes back here to visit you, will you give me a call? It's very important that we speak with him," Detective Hunt said as she gave Lily her business card.

"I will, dear."

"Please do," Detective Hunt continued. "We'll be in touch. Have a nice a day."

"You ladies do the same," Lily said.

As Winnie and Detective Hunt stood up and began to walk to their car, Johnny's black SUV pulled into the driveway.

"There's Johnny now, actually. How lucky!" Lily said.

Winnie and Detective Hunt continued to walk towards their car. They wanted to be able to speak with Johnny without Johnny's grandma hearing. Johnny parked his SUV next to Detective Hunt's car. All four doors of his SUV opened, and Johnny exited along with the PeNabs and four women dressed ready for a nightclub.

"Hey, PeNab!" Johnny said, ignoring Detective Hunt and Winnie completely. "Grab the disco ball."

The PeNabs and women continued into the house and shut the door behind them.

"Johnny Santoro?" Detective Hunt questioned.

"Who wants to know?"

"I'm Detective Hunt, and this is Winnie."

"Good for you."

"Would you mind if we asked you a couple questions?"

"Am I under arrest or something?"

"No," Detective Hunt said.

"Well then you can both fuck off," he responded.

"That is no way to speak to your elders, young man," Winnie said.

"Aren't you a little old to be a cop, lady?"

"It doesn't matter if I'm a police officer or not. You should never speak that way to your elders. It is rude and unnecessary, and if you had a decent bone in your body, you would apologize this instant."

"Go fuck yourself."

"Does Lily know you speak that way? Maybe I'll ask her."

"No, no...that won't be necessary," Johnny hung his head and continued. "I'm sorry, ma'am."

"It's okay, dear. It's just very unbecoming of you to speak that way."

"So may we ask you a couple of questions, Johnny? It will only take a minute," Detective Hunt asked again.

"No," Johnny said, leaving off the foul language. "Now, if you'll excuse me, I'm going to go set up for a special lady's 100th birthday party."

Johnny turned around and walked towards the house.

"Do you know where Beau Allen is?" Winnie asked.

Johnny froze in his tracks and turned around.

"Never heard of the guy."

"Your grandma said you two were good friends."

"I don't know if the two of you noticed, but my grandma is two days away from being 100 years old. She doesn't know what the hell she's talking. I've never heard of the guy," he stated emphatically. "Now, if you'll excuse me."

"Of course," Detective Hunt said. "Let's go, Winnie."

"But, dear!" Winnie whispered.

"It's okay, Winnie," she responded.

Winnie and Detective Hunt got in their car, put it in reverse and backed out of Johnny's Grandma's driveway. Johnny tensely watched their car until it disappeared, and then turned towards the house.

"He's lying!" Winnie said the instant they pulled away.

"I know, Winnie. I know."

"Well what are we going to do? He knows where my Beau is! I know it!"

"I think so too, Winnie."

"Well let's do something, dear!"

Detective Hunt stared at her steering wheel, trying to decide on what action to take. After a good 15 seconds of letting her anger boil up inside, she spoke...

"You're right, Winnie. Johnny is lying - two can play that game."

Detective Hunt picked up her phone and dialed a number.

"Yes, it's Detective Hannah Hunt. I needed a warrant for 156 Valley view Drive. Jersey City, New Jersey, 07302. The house belongs to one Liliana Santoro. She's the grandmother of Johnny Santoro, suspected Captain of Arnaldo Soldetti's crime family. We need this warrant within the hour. We have reason to believe that both Johnny Santoro and Arno Soldetti are currently at the house holding someone hostage. I repeat - Arno Soldetti, boss of the Soldetti Crime family, is at the house, holding someone hostage. We also have reason to believe that this house is being used as the stash house for both their drug and gambling money."

After a few moments, Detective Hunt spoke again.

"That's correct...that's correct. Okay, we'll be there in 30 minutes."

"We're heading back to the station to pick up the search warrant for Lily's house, Winnie."

"That's terrific, dear. That seemed rather easy to me."

"All it took was dropping Arno Soldetti's name. There are some people who have been chasing after him for a long time."

"And you think he has drug money at the house, dear?"

"Maybe. It will get their attention. Our little secret," Detective Hunt replied.

"Well, today, we're going to get him, sweetie!"

"Yes we are, Winnie," Detective Hunt continued, "Yes we are."

When Winnie and Detective Hunt arrived at the police station, there was a team waiting for them, armed and ready to execute the search warrant of Johnny's Grandma's house. They began to load up into police cars and trucks. Winnie went to open the passenger side door of Detective Hunt's car, but Detective Hunt stopped her.

"Winnie," Detective Hunt said, "I'm sorry, but I'm going to have to insist that you stay here at the station during the raid. It's just too dangerous. The ride along simply isn't allowed during raids."

"But..."

"I'm sorry, Winnie, but this is non-negotiable. You have to stay here. These men are armed and dangerous. I will call you the minute we have secured the house."

Winnie was disappointed, but grateful and optimistic.

"Okay, dear. Go save my Beau."

"You saved your Beau, Winnie."

"Thank you, sweetie."

To Winnie's dismay, she returned to Detective Hunt's office, as nervous as she could be, and waited for the call.

Chapter XXVIV

FINGER DIPS

When Johnny joined Arno, the PeNabs, the girls and Beau in the basement, he pulled Arno to the side.

"Hey boss man," Johnny continued. "There was a detective in the driveway asking about Beau."

"What?" Arno asked.

"A detective was asking about Beau," he whispered.

"What'd you tell them?"

"I told her that I didn't know a thing, and that I'd never met him, obviously."

"That's good," Arno said.

"But," Johnny continued. "She did say that my grandma mentioned to her that Beau and I were friends."

"Lily gave a cop information! What the fuck!" Arno said.

"I know. That's not like her. She's getting old, boss," Johnny replied.

"She is getting old," Arno confirmed.

"So what do you think? Should we continue?" Johnny asked.

"Absolutely. If they're just now starting to ask questions, then they're way too late. Let's get fucked up," Arno said.

"Okay then."

Arno walked towards me and tossed the bag of molly on the table.

"Johnny," Arno said. "Put some music on.

"Something funky," I yelled.

"Okay, ladies. It's bright and early - let's party," they cheered as Arno continued. "You may have noticed our tied up and shirtless friend, Beau. Beau's going through a bit of an initiation, if you will, but he is 100% involved of this party. Don't forget that. He may not be able to stand up, but that doesn't mean you shouldn't dance with him. Beau, these are the girls. They work at the club. Say hello."

"Hello, ladies," I said.

"Hi, Beau!" they responded.

"Great, now, Beau, what's the best way to do this stuff?

"Do what stuff?"

"The molly."

"Finger dips."

"Finger dips?"

"Lick your finger, dunk it in the bag and then lick your finger again."

"Okay, Beau-diddly. You first - all five fingers."

"All five? I normally only do two fingers tops."

"On both hands."

"Both hands?"

"I don't think he should do that much," one of the girls said.

"He's got a high tolerance," Arno replied, before he leaned in and whispered. "And it's your going away party - so party."

I had no clue how much molly would actually make me overdose. I just hoped that it would take more than 10 finger dips.

"Let me get my right hand loose at least."

"After what happened the last time you had a hand loose? No chance, Beau," Arno said. "Girls, come give Beau some finger dips."

"I guess that works, too," I replied.

Girl after girl and finger after finger, I ate the molly. It tasted bitter and terrible in a good way.

"Okay, everyone help yourselves," Arno said.

The PeNabs went first. Each of them took two finger dips.

"You sure, boss?" Johnny asked.

"Absolutely."

Johnny took two finger dips. "This taste like shit."

"Worth it," I said.

"Ladies," Arnos invited. They each mingled to the bag and took a finger dip or two. "And now two for me."

It only took about three songs for the heat wave of molly to smack me in the face. It was similar to what I had experienced in the past, but much more intense. I felt a layer of cold sweat over my entire body. The room felt like it was 100 degrees. The music sounded as if it were coming out in slow motion. When I turned my head, my vision trailed. Voices echoed, and for the life of me, I could not stop my feet from dancing. I tried to ask for water, but just as I had the sentence on the tip of my tongue, another heat wave flowed through my body. I laid my head back and shut my eyes. I fell into a trance with the music. Each song blended into the last, completely cancelling my concept of time.

I awoke when the music abruptly stopped. I lifted my head and opened my eyes. I had no idea what was happening or how long it had been happening for. The girls were running up the stairs. Johnny and the PeNabs grabbed a couple duffle bags and ran out after the girls.

"Beau?" Arno echoed, "You with us, buddy?"

"Water," I said.

Arno reached and grabbed a cup of water, and launched it into my face.

"Listen to me, Beau," he began. "I've gotta' shoot you."

"Come on, man. Don't do that," I said as I laid my head back down.

"Beau, snap out of it, dammit."

"Put the music back on."

"We don't have time for that, Beau."

"There's always time for that," I responded.

"Beau!" Arno screamed.

"I'll listen if you hit the music on," I said.

"Dammit, Beau," Arno yelled. Moments later, the music came back on.

"You've got my full attention," I said as I lifted my head and opened my eyes.

"The cops are on their way here right now. I don't leave witnesses behind...ever. It's nothing personal. Deep down...I like ya'. You're an okay dude, but you're also a witness."

"I'm not a witness."

"What do you mean?"

"I didn't witness anything."

"You're a missing person, Beau. They're going to be asking questions when they come down here. I gotta shoot ya'."

Wheels started turning in my head.

"No you don't. I didn't witness anything."

"If you don't figure out a way to make sense on your next sentence you're getting a head shot."

"I did the Omertà," I said.

"Omertà?"

I lifted my head and looked Arno in the eyes, "I already made my Omertà for this entire situation. That means something to me. I'm not going to say a word."

"I don't know, Beau," Arno continued. "How could you possibly talk your way out of this?"

"Get out of here. I'll tell them Johnny's grandma and I are lovers."

"You're what?"

"I'm here on my own free will. Johnny's grandma and I were about to have an intimate session - eating molly and having sex and whatnot."

"You and Johnny's Grandma?"

"That's right. What's her name?" I asked.

"Lily," Arno said as he scratched his chin, pondering the situation. "What about your wounds?"

"It's a sex thing."

"A sex thing?"

"That's right."

"Whose molly is that?"

"Mine."

"Who am I?" He asked.

"No clue."

"What's my name?"

"I don't know."

"Have you ever seen me before?"

"No."

"Are you sure?"

"Positive. I'm telling you, I've got this."

"You'll get some prison time for that much molly," he said as he pointed to it with his gun.

"It's karma. I probably deserve a bit of prison time after all the shit I've done."

"You'd do 10 years?"

"I'll do whatever they give me."

"You sure about that?"

"Omertà."

Arno paused and stared deep into my eyes, hoping to see my true intentions. "I'm going to let you live, Beau."

"Fuck yeah."

"Shut the fuck up for a minute - this needs to be quick. Here's what's going to happen. I'm going to have my lawyer, Taylor Boyd, represent you - on the house. He's a young guy from North Carolina, about your age, actually."

"I don't know if I'd necessarily trust a guy like me in the court room."

"He's fucking ruthless in the courtroom. He's a shark on the golf course, too. He's got quite a few of my guys off the hook completely when they got pinched. This also means that if you even think about taking a deal and name-dropping, you'll be fucked. Do you know what I mean when I say that you'll be fucked?"

"I do."

"Let me clarify, just in case. It means that your entire family will be murdered before someone I have on the inside murders you slowly. Someone will castrate you. You will be fucked. Do you understand?"

"I understand."

"Second - if you stay true to your word and take the prison time, you'll be protected on the inside. You won't have to worry about a thing. It will be the easiest time you can possibly do."

"No way! Fuck yeah. Now I'm actually kind of excited. It's a new life experience."

"Don't make me regret this, Beau. If you come through and do your time, when you get out - all of your debts will be forgiven. If you become a rat, then your problems will be much, much worse."

"I'll come through."

Arno leaned forward and untied me.

"What about Lily?" I asked.

"She'll go along with it. Trust me. She's about to be 100 years old...she won't get any time."

Arno extended his right hand out. I grabbed it and shook.

"I gotta' tell ya', Beau. It makes me feel better that you have a firm handshake. If you had shaken my hand like a dead fish I would've killed you on the spot. That handshake saved your life. Thank your Dad for teaching you that."

"I will."

Arno sprinted out of the basement. A smile spread across my face. I untied my feet, and my smile grew wider. I stood up, and the smile grew wider. Before I knew it, I was grooving to the music. Slight molly waves started rolling through my body again. I leaned over for one last finger dip. When I looked up, I saw Johnny's Grandma walking down the steps.

"Who's here?" she asked.

"It's me, Beau Allen."

"Beau Allen? Where have I heard that name?"

"Listen, Johnny's Grandma. The cops are about to be here."

"Beau Allen…I remember! The cops were looking for you!" She continued as she slowly walked down the basement stairs. "Your grandma was looking for you! Where'd Johnny and the boys run off to in a hurry?" She asked

"Lily, the cops are about to be here. Johnny said it's of utmost importance that you go along with whatever I tell the cops. Okay?"

 "Johnny said that?"

"He did. Now listen, we're in an intimate relationship."

"I'm flattered, Beau, but you're not really my type."

"Seriously? Why not?"

"I'm not a fan of mustaches."

"Well, you should be, but I don't have time to get into that. We're in an intimate relationship. You don't know anything about the drugs. They're mine."

"Drugs?" she asked.

"Drugs," I said as I pointed to the bag of molly on the table. "Do you understand?"

"Of course I understand. These are the type moments made me fall for my husband, Johnny. I feel young again!"

BAM!

The upstairs door was bashed open. There was a stampede of feet rushing through the house.

"NYPD! WE HAVE A WARRANT!"

"By the way, it's my 100th birthday in two days."

"I know - that's so awesome! Are you going to get on the *Smucker's* jar?" I asked.

"I think so!" She said as a smile lit up her face.

"Congratulations!" I said. "You deserve it!"

"LIVING ROOM'S CLEAR!"

"BEDROOM'S CLEAR!"

"KITCHEN'S CLEAR!

"BATHROOM'S CLEAR!

"CHECK THE BASEMENT!"

BAM!

The basement door flung open and smashed into the wall.

"I'VE GOT MOVEMENT DOWN HERE," a cop shouted. "LET ME SEE YOUR HANDS! GET ON YOUR KNEES! LET ME SEE YOUR FUCKING HANDS!"

Johnny's grandma and I both lifted our hands in the air.

"We're not armed," I yelled.

"HANDS!" He yelled back.

"She's 99 years old! Be easy!"

More cops stormed down the stairs. "ON YOUR KNEES! GET ON YOUR FUCKING KNEES!" They yelled as they pointed their guns and flashlights in our face.

"She's 99! Don't make her get on her knees!"

"KNEES MOTHERFUCKER!"

I went down to my knees, and Lily followed - very, very slowly.

"SEARCH THE ROOM!"

Cops scurried around the room quickly, shifting their flashlights from place to place, which completely distracted me until I heard...

"DRUGS!"

"Those are mine!" I yelled.

All of the flashlights shifted to my face and blinded me.

"WHAT'S YOUR NAME?" The cop yelled.

"Beau Allen."

"Beau Allen?"

"That's right."

"HE'S ALIVE!" He yelled to the cops on the stairs. They relayed the message. "HE'S ALIVE!" It was followed by another, "HE'S ALIVE!"

"Out of the way! Out of the way!" Detective Hunt yelled as she pushed cops aside.

"Beau Allen?" she asked.

"That's right," I answered.

"Thank God you're alright. I'm Detective Hannah Hunt. We're going to get you out of here safely."

"I don't want to go anywhere," I said.

"What?" she questioned.

"He said the drugs were his," the cop told her.

"The drugs are his? What drugs?"

"Those drugs," he said - pointing at the bag of molly.

She turned back to me confused.

"Lily," she continued. "What's going on here?"

"I'm sorry. I'm so embarrassed."

"She didn't know about the drugs," I said.

"Cocaine?"

"It's Molly."

"What's going on here?" Detective Hunt repeated.

"We're," I continued. "Intimate."

"Excuse me?" she asked.

"We're intimate – borderline in love."

"Lily?" She asked.

"He's telling the truth," she replied.

Detective Hunt paused and glanced over my upper body, which consisted of a bruised face and bandages everywhere.

"What's with the bandages?" She asked.

"I'm into pain," I said.

"Lily?"

"He's into pain," she confirmed.

"You're...into pain?" she asked

"It's a sexual thing, Detective," I said.

"LOWER YOUR WEAPONS," Detective Hunt demanded of the police force.

"Let me get this straight. You two are having an intimate relationship. A 99 year-old and a...how old are you, Beau?"

"27," I said.

"A 99 year-old and a 27 year-old...in an intimate relationship?"

"What are you trying to say?" Lily asked.

"Nothing...nothing," Detective Hunt said. "And...the drugs are yours?"

"Yeah - Lily didn't know anything about the molly. It was going to be her 100th birthday present from me. Sometimes you gotta live a little, you know?"

"You were going to give a 100 year old woman molly?"

"That's right."

"Did you do any of the molly, Lily?" She asked.

"No, I didn't - nor would I have. Beau's thoughtful, but he's not the brightest."

"She's got me there," I said.

"Did you do any of the molly, Beau?"

"I might have had a finger dip or two."

Detective Hunt shook her head. "Lily, where's Johnny?"

"Johnny? He left right after you did earlier today. He was just here to drop off the disco ball for my birthday party."

She shook her head again, "Beau," she began. "Winnie is going to be awfully disappointed."

"Winnie's here?" I asked.

"She's at the police station. She's been in New York for the past week. She's basically been leading the investigation - trying to find you. We feared you were dead. Now she has to find out that you were not only not missing, but you were down here in an intimate relationship with a woman older than she is, doing drugs."

"Hey!" Lily interrupted.

"Sorry, Lily," she said.

"It's my own fault," I said.

"Is it?" She questioned. "Arrest them both."

"What's Lily under arrest for?" I asked.

"Obstruction of Justice," Detective Hunt replied. "She lied to a police officer."

"No, sweetie, I just didn't remember correctly. I'm 99 years-old...remember?"

Detective Hunt stared at both of us. Her face held the look of utter disappointment. She saw right through us, but she couldn't do anything about it.

"Don't put her in handcuffs," Detective Hunt said. "But she's coming to the station for a statement."

The cops helped Lily to her feet and escorted her out. Detective Hunt handcuffed me and walked me up the stairs. The fun was over.

<u>Chapter XXX</u>

LET IT RIDE

Six months later...

I kept my word to Arno. Now, I spend my time in the New Jersey State prison. I gotta' tell you, I was as nervous as I could be when I left Johnny's Grandma's house. Arno's lawyer, Taylor Boyd, was waiting for me when I arrived. I gave my statement, claiming that the molly was all mine, and that Johnny's Grandma and I were having an intimate moment in the basement. I had been at her house on my own free will.

The detectives offered me immunity multiple times if I were to give up Arno and/or Johnny. I insisted that I had no clue what they were talking about. They drilled me with questions about my stab wounds and bullet holes in an attempt to make me slip up and get caught in my own lie, but it was like I said before - stab wounds and bullet holes are just a couple of my sexual fetishes.

The hardest part about that day was seeing Winnie at the police station. She thought that I had been rescued, and then she found out that I had been arrested. She saw right through my lies, but I simply told her that it was something I had to do. She understood. On a brighter note, hugging my Grandma while I was on molly was the most loved I've ever felt. It made no difference to her if I were the President of the United States or just another inmate of the New Jersey State Prison - she loves me all the same, and she visits once per month.

Speaking of months, I was assigned to spend quite a few of them here in the pen. I pleaded guilty - which helped me avoid the whole courtroom deal for the most part. However, they gave me a tough sentence. I had a couple minor possession charges that came back to bite me. That, combined with everyone suspecting that I was covering for a mafia boss, inspired the judge to give me the maximum time possible for my crime. Five years. Up for parole in three. When I originally heard the amount of time that I had to spend locked up, my heart sank. Five years of my life...gone.

When I arrived at the big house, I tried to walk and look tough. Being one of the smallest dudes there – that was no easy task. However, it didn't take long for Arno to keep his word. The first prison guard I saw immediately walked up to me and shook my hand. His name was officer Frank Costa. He told me I could call him Frank. He also told me if I ever need cigarettes, that he was my guy. He walked me to my cellblock and showed me my cell. When I saw where I would be sleeping for the next three to five years, I smiled. It was a single cell. Clutch. The bed had a legitimate mattress on it. All of the other cells had a small pad for a mattress. On top of that, there was a television with a DVD player attached to it in the corner of the cell. There was a curtain around my toilet and sink area. Best of all - it had a mini fridge. Boom. Arno wasn't done making sure that I was comfortable either. Every week I get a random letter, without a return address, that is filled with weed and rolling papers. Let's say it one more time. Clutch.

Frank introduced me to a couple of large Italian gentlemen named Enzo and Sal. They informed me that I had absolutely nothing to fear. That made it much easier to walk tough. I realized that prison was not only doable, but it was an experience that I was looking forward to. Why wouldn't I? I had protection from the Italians and the guards! It gave me a unique opportunity to mingle among New York's most dangerous criminals with immunity. Talk about power.

Speaking of power, it didn't take me long to test it out. During my first prison breakfast, some asshole was chewing his cereal with his mouth wide open and he was smacking his lips. I almost let that go, but then he started slurping the milk from his cereal bowl. It was too much. I asked him to chew with his mouth closed. I even said, "Please." He stood up, threw his tray against a wall and told me to go fuck myself. He spent the next month in the prison's hospital ward. When he got out, he asked to be moved into the prison's protective custody unit. Not too shabby...

Enzo and Sal also introduced me to the man. Leo de Luca. He's a good friend of Arno's, and he runs the show in prison. Leo told me that we'd sit down real soon with some roast beef sandwiches and beer so that I could tell him the stories that Arno had mentioned. I told Leo that it would be an honor. The more mafia bosses you can befriend, the better.

If the protection wasn't enough, Arno took it one step further. He set me up with every prisoners' favorite two words, and he does so once a month. Conjugal visits. That's right. Conjugal visits. For those of you who don't know what those are, it basically means that I get have sex while incarcerated - with women. I've been having more luck in the bedroom in prison that I was having on the outside. Arno suggested to Isabella Rossi that she should visit me. He told her that I was a stand up guy. It's probably the most meaningful thing anyone has ever said about me. Isabella and I hit it off immediately. She's gorgeous, smart and funny. What more can you ask for? For the first four conjugal visits, we just talked and got to know each other. We both felt a connection. Then, there was the fifth conjugal visit..

By far the most underrated aspect about my stint in prison is that I'm now able to play a major sympathy card with my parents. They've come up to visit three times. Each time I see them I greatly exaggerate how hard life is inside the slammer. They don't know about my sweet setup. They encourage me to stay strong. I think they respect me more now than they ever did before. It turns out that surviving in prison doesn't just get you street cred on the streets, but it carries over to your home as well. Also, my dad is scared of me now – which is awesome.

I'd be lying if I said there were no struggles for me inside the joint. The main one is my gambling addiction is thriving. I won five cartons of cigarettes last week. I don't know what the fuck I'm going to do with five cartons of cigarettes. I don't even smoke. But regardless, I won them, which is nice. I might throw all five cartons on a bet soon. That's a large wager in prison. Sometimes you just have to go big.

While that strategy may have ultimately landed me in prison, it also gave me plenty of time to discover who I am. It helped me find my voice – which may be the single most important discovery a person can make in their lifetime. It lets them stand up and yell confidently for what they believe in. Personally - I believe in letting it ride - in every aspect of life.

Go with the flow. Trust your gut. Make impulsive decisions - they're always the most fun. Live without regrets. If that's not possible - just remember that regretting something you did is always better than regretting something you didn't do. Experience a genuine rush at least once a year. Be confident. Like yourself. Get punched in the face at least once. Get naked in public. Travel. Don't be afraid of change. Listen to funky music. Laugh. Drink good beer. Be happy. Have fun. Love your grandma. And when the vibe is just right – let it ride.

43380656R00149

Made in the USA
Lexington, KY
27 July 2015